Marilyn Anderson,
April, 2000

DAKOTA INCARNATE

DAKOTA INCARNATE

A Collection of Short Stories

Bill McDonald

For Don Eid,
You should write too,

Bill McDonald

Minnesota Voices Project
Number 92
New Rivers Press 1999

Cover and interior design and typesetting by Steve Canine
Printed in Canada

New Rivers Press is a nonprofit literary press dedicated to
publishing the very best emerging writers in our region,
nation, and world.

The publication of *Dakota Incarnate* has been made
possible by generous grants from the Jerome Foundation;
the North Dakota Council on the Arts; and Dayton's,
Mervyn's California, and Target Stores by the Dayton
Hudson Foundation.

Additional support has been provided by the General Mills
Foundation, the McKnight Foundation, the Star Tribune
Foundation, and the contributing members of New
Rivers Press.

New Rivers Press
420 North Fifth Street
Minneapolis, MN 55401

*This book is dedicated to my grandparents
Jeremiah and Mary Ann Lyons and to all of
the other pioneers who homesteaded the Dakota
prairies and built lasting communities there.
Their valor, industry, and humanity represent
one of the finest chapters of American history.*

*The book is further dedicated to my wife,
Lois, who has taken an interest in it and has
improved it with helpful suggestions and
meticulous copyediting.*

Contents

ACKNOWLEDGMENTS

Some of the stories in this collection were originally published as part of the author's thesis for the master of fine arts degree, Department of English, specialty in creative writing, Mankato State University, December 1995.

Dakota: Where Stories like These Could Happen

The rise and fall of community in rural Dakota over the past 120 years is a poignant story. Dakota Territory, a vast land of waving grass and audacious men and women, ceased to exist in 1889, when North and South Dakota were carved out of it and made into states. Dakota as a concept, however, lived on, and lives still.

The area was first settled in a huge rush sponsored by the railroads, generally during 1878–1887. During this turbulent era, fraud was rampant, much of the land was acquired by speculators for later resale to real settlers, and many towns grew and died out to nothing again within a few years. Prohibition, women's suffrage, and statehood were major political issues. Women's suffrage failed to pass by a single vote in the territorial legislature in 1872, forty-six years before it finally became reality.

Many early settlers were ill prepared, and the droughts of 1888–1890 drove them from Dakota. The suffrage issue was on the ballot in November 1890, the year following statehood. A pitched battle erupted, involving national figures such as Susan B. Anthony and Dr. Anna Shaw, who wrote as follows:

> That South Dakota campaign was one of the most difficult we ever made. It extended over nine months; and it was impossible to describe the poverty which prevailed throughout the whole rural community of the State. There had been three consecutive years of drought. The sand was like powder, so deep that the

wheels of the wagons in which we rode "across country" sank half-way to the hubs; and in the midst of this dry powder lay withered tangles that had once been grass. Every one had the forsaken desperate look worn by the pioneer who had reached the limit of his endurance, and the great stretches of prairie roads showed innumerable canvas-covered wagons, drawn by starved horses, and followed by starved cows, on their way "Back East."

But many settlers persevered, and better times followed the initial turmoil. Railroads and roads crisscrossed the country; towns, churches, and schools were built; and rural Dakota prospered. By the time of World War I the earliest settlers had been there for forty years, and the prairie had been transformed into an energetic, young community.

Some of the children of the pioneers were going from country school to college, and returning to their communities as teachers, lawyers, doctors, ministers, and priests. Farms had come to be of a size suitable for their locale, and passable roads led to well-kept farms and to rural schools and churches. Enthusiasm and optimism were the order of the day.

Small towns were at the hub of such communities. Every small town had a bank, a doctor, a drug store, a hotel, a grain elevator, and a railroad depot.

But these small towns and, to some extent, the communities they served were doomed by progress, and by the dust bowl and the depression of the thirties. When automobiles became common, the small towns began to dry up. Most South Dakota farmers lost their farms in the thirties, and depopulation began as people left for California. Taken as a whole, the population of South Dakota is essentially the same now as it was in 1930. But the state was only 16 percent urban then—it is 50 percent urban now.

When times improved again, farms became larger. A decreased farm population and the availability of buses and cars put an end to the country school and the country church. The trend toward larger farms accelerated as large machinery took over.

Superficially, a rural Dakota neighborhood today may seem to be little changed from 1915. The same road net is there, and groves of trees mark the same farmstead sites that they did eighty years earlier.

A closer look, however, reveals that the farm buildings on those sites are gone or stand in ruins. A barn may linger on the site, sheltering livestock that belongs to a farmer who lives five miles away. Often there is nothing except a few old foundations and a dim track through the grass that was once a driveway.

Even the railroads are gone. The tracks and ties have been torn up and hauled away. The fences that enclosed the right-of-way are gone, and, in places, even the grade itself has been bulldozed away and leveled. Corn waves in the wind where the eleven-thirty passenger once made its daily run.

The schools are gone too, most of them without a trace. The fences around the playgrounds were taken down; the buildings, along with their meager foundations, were removed; and the land was plowed over.

For those of us who knew those schools, there is something ghostly about the sites now. The surroundings appear to be unchanged, the same roads, the same fields, the same farmsteads off in the distance. But the school, the center of it all—gone somehow. It is like a dream. The school should be right here—here where all of the feet trod, day after day, where the bell rang, the children shouted, the teacher read; here where we put up blankets and sheets to make a stage for Christmas programs and here where the county superintendent of schools came to visit. How can it not be here? Everything else is the same. Actually, of course, nothing is the same except the road and the field. The farmstead, if you go closer, stands empty and deserted, the buildings gone or falling down. The children are old men and women, many of them dead and buried; there have been no shouts of children here for fifty years.

To a great extent, the silence that reigned over the Dakota prairie before the settlers came has returned to claim its own. A culture has come and gone. That culture was brief, but it was rich, as pioneer cultures often are. Men and women loom larger than life when they share the opening of a new land.

This book aims to preserve a few samples of that culture for its reader. *Dakota Incarnate* contains four short stories: "Rosebud Requiem," "David's Drummer," "The Essay Contest," and "Dakota Reincarnation." The stories are set in what is now South Dakota and relate to that area at various times from the 1870s until the present. All four pieces of fiction rely heavily upon real episodes from Dakota history.

"Rosebud Requiem" is set in 1910 in the former Rosebud Indian Reservation after that land had been purchased by the federal government and opened to homesteaders. The plot line for this story, however, was suggested by an earlier incident in another part of western South Dakota.

"David's Drummer" is drawn from a history that is unique to South Dakota—that of the Hutterites. This small, German-speaking religious sect came to Dakota Territory from the Ukraine in the 1870s and established communes on the prairie. Their ways of life and of farming were successful, and they expanded and established new colonies until World War I, when religious prejudice and misguided patriotism drove them from the state.

"The Essay Contest" is set in eastern South Dakota in 1935 and relates the day-to-day experiences of a farm boy named Jackie.

"Dakota Reincarnation" is set in 1993, but the plot involves a man who homesteaded in Dakota Territory in the 1870s. Jer Lyons died in 1893, but he mysteriously returns to life a hundred years later and, with his sixty-nine-year-old grandson, revisits the Dakota he had known in the previous century.

These stories are not presented as history. One of the historian's most important tasks is to present a balanced account of an era. A history book can describe only a select few of the many, many episodes that occurred. The historian must choose episodes that truly represent the larger picture.

Even twenty-four hundred years ago, the problems involved in doing this were appreciated by the Greek historian Herodotus. The episode that is exactly right to properly convey the correct impression of the whole is often elusive. As with a piece about the average American family, a family with 2.63 children, it is hard to find a representative example. Herodotus argued that the historian was entitled, even obligated, to create his own episode.

"Very few things happen at the right time, and the rest do not happen at all," he said. "The conscientious historian will correct these defects." Modern historians do not feel so free.

Writers who blend history into fiction have a less rigorous task. They have an obligation to be true to the facts in any history they use as background, but they have no obligation to be complete. Many writers even feel free to distort history or to create bogus history as long as it is done is such a way that a reasonable reader will recognize it as fiction.

Writers of fiction have a different focus than historians do. Their focus is not upon events but on people. They speak from the perspective of their characters. The criterion is not whether the experiences of the characters are typical of an era, or whether they really happened, but whether they could reasonably have happened, given the way things were in the time and place where the story is set.

If they could have happened, they probably did happen, according to one view. Fyodor Dostoevsky says that the "notes" in his *Notes from the Underground* are fictional. "Nevertheless," he adds, "such persons as the author of such memoirs not only may, but must, exist in our society."

Many works of fiction are tied closely to real events and people. The plays of William Shakespeare are an example. Plutarch's *Lives of the Noble Romans* was first translated into French. A later English translation of the French work was so heavily drawn upon by the Bard that it became known as "Shakespeare's Source Book." Yet Shakespeare's plays enrich our understanding of that era far beyond the meager facts given us by Plutarch.

These stories are meant to serve two purposes. I hope the modern reader will suffer, exult, and ponder along with Annie, David, Jer, Tom, and Ellen—that she or he will share the lives of these people in full measure and live beside them as they make their way through these stories. In the process, I also hope my reader will come away with a better understanding of a world that is gone now.

ROSEBUD
REQUIEM

The Mailbox

"Well, at least, goddam it, I've got a mailbox."

Tom Fleming said this to himself. He was not a morose man who preferred conversation with himself to conversation with others, but there were no others. Well, yes, there were his horses.

Gypsy often seemed sympathetic when they came dragging back to the claim shanty after a long, hot day spent breaking sod with the plow. She would rub her huge soft head against his back and side as he was pulling the bridle bit from Buster's mouth.

Gypsy's caresses were meant to be gentle, but they often plastered Tom up against Buster's collar and hames, and sometimes threatened to root him right up off the ground and over the gelding's neck. Buster was older and less demonstrative. His eye was on the water tank, and on the barnyard (still barnless) where he could roll in the dust once Tom pulled the harness from his sweat-drenched body. Buster wasn't much for company, but he was a good horse all the same. A hell of a good horse.

Tom didn't talk much with Buster, beyond giddap and whoa, but he sometimes poured his heart out to Gypsy. She was a beautiful young sorrel mare, weighed close to eighteen hundred pounds, and had the softest skin imaginable. Her golden mane and tail would often glisten and glow like two parts of a sun-lit stream as they flowed in the wind. Gypsy had huge eyes of the softest brown, flaring nostrils, and a muzzle like velvet. It was impossible not to love her. Life on the homestead was hard, but Tom had his dreams, and he told Gypsy about them as he curried and brushed her, or fitted her into the harness.

The dream that obsessed him was the dream that he would have a wife with him here someday. Waking or sleeping, this dream haunted him. It took many forms—he saw her, he saw himself, they were going through life together.

Sometimes, in the dream, they were middle-aged. The crude claim shanty had been replaced by a distinguished two-story white house with a gambrel roof. They stood on the porch, behind the railing. His arm was comfortably around her waist, she was leaning against him, they were looking out at their lush fields that stretched away into the distance. A big, red, hipped-roof barn stood to the right, surrounded by white-faced cattle and by horses that looked a lot like Gypsy.

Another time—it was after one of his evening meals of fried oatmeal—the dream was different. They were younger, not much older than he was now. The new house hadn't been built yet, the tiny gray claim shanty still stood there, but it had been fixed up a little bit, somehow. He was coming in from the field after a brutal day in the sun and wind. He had put the horses away and headed toward the house. As he neared the door, his nose caught a tantalizing, familiar odor. The nose knows. It never forgets. It was impossible, but it was his mother's pork pie. That memory, and that odor, were from his happy childhood on the farm near Mankato. But his mother had died when he was twelve.

He burst in and kissed his wife; she smiled and motioned him to the table.

There were other dreams too. Dreams too private to tell Gypsy about, or to be uttered aloud. They came to him often, over and over. In these dreams he held his wife, caressed her, marveled at the whiteness of her body, buried his face in her breasts. Tom was twenty-one and had never had a woman, but he had an imagination about it. She touched him too, in those dreams, touched him with her body, her hands. Finally, in his blankets on the dirt floor of the claim shanty, it would be his own hand that did the touching, and then he could sleep.

In his stronger moments Tom scorned himself for being weak. He knew that, during their first years, many earlier homesteaders had endured vigils more lonely than his. Some family groups had staked claims in the fall, built and provisioned a claim shanty, and then left one man alone there to watch the claims through the winter. The others had returned to civilization. One guy he had heard of sat in and around his claim shack from the sixteenth of November until the twenty-fourth of March without ever seeing another human being. That was in 1878 in Dakota Territory, near what is now Huron. "Slept most of the time," reported that gentleman of his ursine odyssey.

This was not 1878. This was 1910, and Tom was in the Rosebud. "The Rosebud" was the former Rosebud Indian Reservation, home of the Rosebud Sioux. It was in South Dakota, along the Nebraska border, west of the Missouri River—a vast area of marginal land formerly used for cattle grazing.

It should have been left that way. The big cattle companies paid fifteen cents per head per year to graze cattle there, and the money went to the Indians, or supposedly did. Actually, it went to the Indian Tribal Fund to be used to buy houses, cattle, and horses for the Indians as the BIA in Washington saw fit. In contrast to most deals between the Indians and the BIA, this worked out fairly well by all accounts.

Some old maps show this area as part of "The Great American Desert," but there had been some wet years, and a great clamor arose to buy the reservation from the Indians and open it for homesteading. A fight erupted, but the promoters had their way. A bill, in the form of a treaty with the Rosebud Sioux, finally passed, and President McKinley signed it in a hoopla ceremony with all of the western congressmen. Each Indian of one-eighth blood received an allotment of 160 acres. The homesteader paid six dollars per acre plus a small fee. The six dollars went to the Indian; Uncle Sam kept the administrative fee.

Applications to buy flooded the land office from all over the country, so the government set up a lottery to pick those who would be allowed to buy. Tom was one of the "winners" in Tripp County. His aim was to actually develop a farm and home on his claim. Many other winners were mere speculators, anxious to sell.

Tom had a few neighbors who lived within a mile or two of him, but he saw little of them. It had always been hard for him to meet people, and the few that he knew here seemed strange to him. They were busy with work and family, and they were Scandinavians who hung together. Tom worked and dreamed and talked to Gypsy.

The spring mud was gone by early May, so Tom took the team and wagon into Gregory one day for supplies. They had started out at sunrise. It was about twenty miles away, and the town wasn't much when you got there. Gregory was fairly new, and located in the first part of the Rosebud to be opened. It had a post office, though, and some fairly good suppliers.

Tom had stepped into the saloon while he was there, and he saw a flyer on the wall that got his attention immediately. The era of mail-order wives was pretty well over by then, but the Rosebud gave it a little revival.

"Lonesome?" asked the flyer.

"You got it," thought Tom.

"Five bucks," it said. His name and thirty-word statement would be furnished "to such of the agency's clients as had expressed interest." They would be free to contact him directly by mail, if interested. Tom headed for the post office.

He edited his text carefully before consigning it to an envelope with a five-dollar money order. The final draft read as follows:

> Twenty-one-year-old Irish Catholic farmer on Rosebud homestead with Minnesota farm background longs for wife and partner. Good prospects for a hard-working couple here.

He wished he had room to mention something about what the homestead was like now. But what can you do in thirty words? He sent it off.

Next, he talked with the postmaster about a mailbox; he had heard that there was rural free delivery of some kind. There was. Once-a-week delivery. The RFD route was along an east-west trail that passed Tom's farm three miles to the north of it. He could put up a box there. The mailman went that way every Thursday. Usually.

Tom went back to the mercantile to add a mailbox to his order. Soon after that, he and Gypsy and Buster were headed back west toward the claim. On the way he dropped the mailbox and a post off at the spot where it was to stand. Darkness was falling, he would have to come back tomorrow with a spade, and hammer and nails, to set it up.

He was there now, leaning on his spade and surveying the finished job. It gave him a feeling that he was connected with the world, seeing his mailbox standing there. It was a little like home, like the farm back in Minnesota. People came by here. Every week, for sure—probably almost every day. With a sigh, he put the spade over his shoulder and started the long walk back.

"Well, at least, goddam it, I've got a mailbox," said Tom Fleming.

Milwaukee

"You're to take the four-horse hitch down to Fulton Street today, Dan," said Mr. Jacobs. "Watch that those kegs are well lashed. That street is a mess from the gas pipe work down there, and you know what the Milwaukee Street Department is like. The load is all fifty-gallon kegs, twenty of 'em, so you'll have near five ton on. The saloon Jacks can help you unload. You know the route?"

"McGinty's, Sullivan's, Gunderson's, the Emporium," answered Dan Thomas. "Then through the alley to catch that pool hall and from there come down behind Egan Avenue to the dock for Schroeder and Olson. I'll be rid of most of the load by then, so I can pull Standorfer's hill and catch those three places on Owen Street. It'll take me most of the day."

"I expect it will," said Jacobs. "Is your daughter working today?"

"She'll be in at nine," said Dan. "She's working six hours now. If I'm late getting back, tell her to wait. We can take the streetcar home together." The sun was climbing up over Lake Michigan as he walked through the warehouse on his way to the barn to harness his horses.

Dan got back to the plant early, unloaded his empties, and spent a little time on the wagon. "Those wheels could use some grease," he thought, and he had to hunt for the jack and break out a new bucket of axle grease in order to attend to it. He finished just in time to meet Ellen as she came out of the plant.

"Hi, Pa," she said, taking his arm. She was eighteen, but she still called him Pa. He liked that.

Ellen was fidgeting with her handbag and pursing her lips as they walked along, Dan noticed. Her eyes were everywhere but on his. Perhaps she had something to tell him. He puzzled over what it might be. Well, they would have forty-five minutes on the car, she could tell him then. It was good that they often had this ride together. She was a plain girl and seemed to be lonely since her mother had died. His sister took good care of the house now and was good company for him, but she and Ellen seemed to be like strangers to each other.

The Shaker Heights car clanked to a stop in front of them, and they stepped up onto the rear platform. Dan greeted the conductor, who was a member of his lodge, and dropped two tokens into the slot. "Good afternoon, Mr. Murphy," said Ellen. She and her father took a seat together on the left side of the aisle.

"Out with it then, girl," said Dan, as the car gathered speed. Ellen smiled and bumped her forehead against his shoulder. "It's terrible how you see through me all the time." She turned from him to look out the window for a moment, then turned back and took his forearm in both of her hands. "I do want to talk to you."

Ellen opened her purse, searched around for a second, and pulled out a small folded piece of gray paper. Turning from Dan, she opened it and read carefully. Then she folded it again and turned back. With her eyes on the floor, she thrust it into his hand; then she braced herself back into a corner with clenched fists and lowered head.

Tom's penciled message from Gregory had been set into rough type on a gray three-by-five-inch card, and his name and address had been added. Ellen had paid three dollars for it. The message had an impersonal feel to it, now that this ragged type had replaced Tom's careful handwriting.

Dan read it with a start and then hastily read it again. He glanced toward Ellen huddled into her corner, looked all around the car for an answer, cleared his throat, focused in, and slowly read it a third time. Then he put it on his lap and grew thoughtful as his eyes misted over. After that he reached over to squeeze Ellen's hand before picking up the message for a fourth perusal. This time he turned it over and studied the back as well, but he could find nothing there. Finally, he nodded slowly and handed the paper back to Ellen. Like most people, Dan knew about the Rosebud. "Tell me more about this," he said.

"It's an excitement for me, Pa," said Ellen. "Except for you, I'm getting to be lonesome and alone here now. I don't want to be an old maid at the brewery."

Dan nodded. He understood what his daughter was saying and that she was right about the alone part. Since she had finished school she had lost touch with most kids her age from the neighborhood. They were an empty-headed lot, anyway, and were falling into dissipation or into habitual, mindless routine. He wanted new friends for his plain, sensitive child, but she had become a woman. She had a type of beauty too, but only older people saw it. He could understand why an idea like this would appeal to her, and he could see some possibilities in it.

Instinctively, though, Dan saw trouble. Ellen was reserved, but her world had always been filled with people. She had always had the neighborhood, the church, the school—and now the brewery. She had no close friends, but she had many friends and moved among them in a pleasant way. She had always lived where things were taken care of by others—this streetcar that they were riding in, the tracks it ran on, the street, the school, the church, the house, the brewery. She could have no concept of a world where there was only the prairie and you—none of the human institutions, no one to take care of anything. It would shock her, and Dan thought he knew his daughter well enough to think that it would never work well for her.

"Do you know anything else about this man?" he asked.

She did not. The letter had only come two days ago. They sat and pondered, father and daughter together. "Well," said Dan, "if you want to go further with it, you must begin by getting some references. Even if there is no one else out there, he says that he is Catholic, and has a Minnesota farm background. There must be family, or a priest, that would know about him."

They both sat silent and thoughtful while the car halted at the Elm Street crossing and new passengers milled in the aisle. Then Dan spoke again. "The main thing is, don't commit yourself until you know enough about it. If the references seem all right and you want to go further, you could maybe take the train out there to meet him and look at the place, or something. Even then, though, you'd want it to be clear that you've only agreed to come and look. One step at a time"

Ellen was relieved. And thoughtful. And excited. Already, in her mind, she was composing her first letter to Tom. What Pa said made sense, she had no disagreement with it—it seemed to settle a lot of things. "I should have thought this through like he did," she said to herself. "I'll have to start doing better about such things." She squeezed her father's arm again and nodded absently. "I'll write to him tonight."

The letter was not finished that night, or the next, although a number of crumpled false starts accumulated in the wastebasket. Ellen was torn between telling and asking, between reticence and candor, and between misgivings and enthusiasm. She learned a lot about herself in writing that letter. Short and pleasant, she finally decided. Her letter would be short and pleasant. It and her mailing address went off in a brown envelope the next day:

> *Milwaukee, Wisconsin*
> *June 7th, 1910*

> *Dear Tom Fleming,*
> *I have your message and would like to hear more about you and your situation. My address is enclosed.*
> *I am eighteen years old. We are also Catholic; I attended the Sister School here through the eighth grade. My father is a teamster for a brewery, and I work there part time.*
> *You can write to our priest here about me if you want to, or others. I can send you addresses. I need the same from you. You mention a Minnesota farm background. Is there a priest in Minnesota that knows you that I could write to?*
> *Please tell me more about yourself, and about the farm and the Rosebud. I have never been on a farm.*

> *Sincerely yours,*
> *Ellen Thomas*

Ellen decided not to show the letter to her father before she mailed it, although she wanted to. "I have to start doing things for myself," she decided.

"I mailed it, Pa," she told him on the streetcar that afternoon.

"Well, don't chew your fingernails off waitin' for something to come back," he said, and returned to his newspaper.

Ex-president Theodore Roosevelt was trying to unite the warring factions of the Republican Party, but seemed to be doing as much harm as good. Napoleon LaJoie of Cleveland and Ty Cobb of the Detroit Tigers were in a hot contest for the American League batting championship. Sun Yat-sen was bringing hopes of freedom to China.

Contact

The magnificent steam locomotive burst out of Chicago, towing that microcosm of 1910 America, the Rock Island Rocket. It wailed its way across northern Illinois and into Iowa, bearing Pullman cars and plush coaches bound for Los Angeles. Traveling salesmen mingled in the bar and talked knowingly of territories. ("You gotta know the territory.") Business tycoons and U.S. senators juggled empires in private cars immediately ahead of the caboose. Society matrons dined in elegance in the dining car, attended by black stewards in gleaming uniforms. Three mail cars followed immediately behind the locomotive and tender, insulating the passengers from the smoke and cinders. In these cars, harried postal clerks sorted mail through the night. The Sioux City mail car was to be switched off at Missouri Valley, and it seemed as if mail for the whole Northwest was being routed through Sioux City now.

The clerks were ready on time, though, and Ellen's brown envelope was sacked with thousands of others on that car when the Omaha-Sioux City train picked it up in Missouri Valley. The sack was shunted to another train in Sioux City, and its contents were sorted into local mail sacks as the pufferbilly snorted along toward Yankton and Pierre. This train hooted its way into Platte, South Dakota, at 1:37 in the afternoon on Monday, June 13, and left the sack with Ellen's letter on the station platform. The mail in the sack had already been presorted into local bundles.

March of 1910 had seen the Missouri River west of Platte in one of its greatest spring floods; it had gorged with ice for eighteen miles and destroyed all of the roads leading to the ferry landings. But this was June, and the Snake Creek Landing ferry was back in full operation. The team and wagon carrying the small sack with Ellen's letter went across the river on that ferry on Tuesday morning, and her letter was delivered to the Gregory post office before nightfall.

Old Palmer Benson was the rural mail carrier out of Gregory. He had two routes and could cover each of them in two days in good weather. He had come in Tuesday night from the Monday route, glad for a chance to spend two nights in a row in his bed. "I'm gettin' too damn old for sleeping on the ground," he muttered.

Palmer had the spring wagon loaded early, and he and his team set off again on Thursday morning. He reached Tom Fleming's mailbox before noon and left Ellen's letter there after looking at the feminine handwriting, sniffing for perfume (there was none), and wondering. It was the second letter he had delivered to that box. The other one had come from Minnesota and had a Fleming name for a return address, so he figured it to be family.

The mailbox had added a new routine to Tom Fleming's life. Thursdays had a new feel, because he was anxious to finish his work early enough to be able to walk the six miles to the mailbox and back before dark. It had been nearly six weeks now, but a dwindling hope for an answer to his message still lingered with him. "This is foolish," he had told himself when he sent it off. "This is foolish," he had repeated to Gypsy many times since, but the hope persisted. His thoughts had been on that hope instead of on his mower that afternoon as he and the team were cutting prairie hay in the draw east of the house, and he had run the sickle into a roll of barbed wire that he had left there. It had broken a sickle section; and he had lost an hour or more in returning to the house, getting the sickle out of the machine, hammering out the broken section, and riveting a new one in its place.

His duties were increasing. He had bought a cow and a few chickens, and had started a garden. The cow was dry, but she had been bred back after her first calf and he expected her to calve again in early July. She was a red roan, seemed to have mostly shorthorn blood. He had finally been able to break her to tether, but he knew that he would have to have her and the calf and the chickens into some kind of shelter before winter. The horses would need at least a windbreak, too, so he had started cutting and hauling tree trunks from the creek bed to the south for posts. He intended to make a kind of a straw shed using prairie hay instead of straw.

It was hard to find enough time because he had been so busy trying to get some crops planted, and both horses were being worked too hard—he could see that. Buster was getting thin, and Gypsy had neck sores from the collar. He worried about those sores, especially with fly time coming on, and put salve on them every night after she had rolled and the sweat had dried from her body.

These thoughts drove him and occupied him day and night, busy day after lonely night. There were many days when his whole enterprise seemed interminable and impossible. The one letter that he did get in the mailbox was from his Aunt Bess in Mankato, really his only relative. She was a hard-eyed woman who had never been close, so he was surprised to hear that she seemed to be concerned for him. It was too much for a boy of his age to do alone, she had insisted. But there was nothing for him in Mankato, he knew that. His parents had died in debt while trying to farm there.

His step was light tonight, though, as he rushed about to finish his chores so that he could head for the mailbox. His one self argued and scolded him for his foolish optimism, and warned him of another bitter disappointment ahead, but his other self could not bear to listen. He hastened through his chores, tethered Buster and Gypsy in some good grass behind the claim shanty, fried two eggs to go with some potatoes he had boiled the night before, and set off for the mailbox about 7:30, as the evening shadows began to lengthen. With six miles to walk he would be back before it got totally dark. Gypsy nuzzled his chest when he checked her halter on the way by. "Wish me luck, girl," said Tom wistfully. She did. He was sure that she had wished it for him.

The sun was setting in glorious red as the mailbox came into sight. The wind had died to a whisper, and night sounds were beginning to rustle the grass. A single red-tailed hawk soared over the rise to the north, eyes intent for a scurrying gopher.

Tom's mood changes abruptly as he faces the final quarter of a mile. His step slows, and agony sweeps over him. Is this really him? Here alone, alone in the universe, day ending, the implacable prairie stretching for miles, forever, away, marked only by two tracks that head through the grass toward the setting sun?

"And my damn mailbox. Look at it. Like a tin can nailed to a scruffy post, yet it has drawn me here like the Sirens luring Odysseus."

For the first time since his mother's funeral nine years earlier, tears stream down Tom's face, and a sob shakes his body.

His composure returns, however, and finally he is at the box. As he pauses to steel himself for its empty interior, his eye falls on the wagon wheel track at his feet. It is fresh. Someone has stopped at his mailbox! He snatches the handle and jerks the cover open, even as his inner voice cautions him—probably Aunt Bess again, if anything.

But the letter is not from Aunt Bess; he sees that at once as he holds the envelope before him. His name, in a neat feminine hand. No return address, but a postmark. Milwaukee, Wisconsin, June 8th, 1910.

The inner voice prates on with additional cautions, but Tom Fleming has sunk into the grass. The last rays of the setting sun see him opening the brown envelope with infinite care.

Plans

> Milwaukee, Wisconsin
> *Thurs., Aug. 4th, 1910*

Dear Tom Fleming,

My trip to come to meet you and see the farm is all arranged if I get a letter from you by Saturday, August 20th, confirming that this schedule is all right. I realize that you will have to get your letter into Gregory without waiting for your mailman to come, but you said that you would be able to do that.

My train leaves Union Depot in Chicago at 10 p.m. on Sunday, August 21st. I have a sleeping berth reserved and can board the train anytime after six, so my father will take me there Sunday evening. My car will be switched to the Sioux City train so I don't have to do anything until I get to Sioux City at six o'clock Monday morning, then I have two hours until I catch the train for Pierre. It gets to Platte, So. Dak., at 1:37 in the afternoon and I have a reservation at the Frontier Hotel there for Monday night. The mail wagon driver is expecting me as a passenger and will pick me up at the hotel at eight o'clock on Tuesday morning. We will cross the Missouri River on the ferry at the "Snake Creek Landing," and he expects to be in Gregory at about three in the afternoon. I have a reservation where you suggested (the Cody Hotel) in Gregory for Tuesday and Wednesday nights, and will start the trip back home on Thursday morning.

I will expect to meet you at the hotel in Gregory on Tuesday evening, and I understand that we will start out very early (you mentioned 4 a.m.) on Wednesday for the farm. Now that I have done all of this the trip itself sounds very exciting. My father offered to come with me, but I said I could do it alone. I think the trip sounds exciting to him too, he has been reading about Dakota and talking to everybody.

I'm very excited about meeting you too, as I'm sure you can guess. I'm glad that you liked my picture, I wish that I had one of you too.

Your Aunt Bess sent me another letter, and Father Mueller had another note from Father Quinlan at Mankato to say that he had found records of both your first communion and your confirmation there. He remembers your mother well, and her early death, but that was nine years ago. He doesn't seem to know a lot about you since, but he says that you were a "good boy" when you were young.

You say that your Aunt Bess is a hard woman, and I'm sure that you know, but she likes you and worries about you. She told me that your parents had died in debt from trying to farm in Minnesota, and I'm sure that such experiences make her act hard. I'm very sorry that you lost your parents that way; my mother died too, and I don't know how I could have lived without my father.

Your aunt wants us to meet, but she is very worried about what you are doing on the Rosebud. I think that, based on years of farming experience, she has almost no hope that your farm can be a success. She told me that she had written to you and tried to convince you that you should find some way to sell it and move back to Minnesota. She thinks it would be better if we met there. Besides that, she thinks that the Rosebud is too lonely for you alone, or even for a young couple alone.

My father is worried too. He has been reading and talking with people about the Rosebud, and has come

to agree with the many people that think it is really part of a desert except during an occasional spell of a few wet years. "The 100th meridian of longitude marks the western limit of profitable farming," he has read. "Nature will have her way, the farms on the Rosebud are doomed," things like that. I'm sure that you have heard all of this.

Another article that he saw claimed that the farming itself would draw the rain—"Rain will follow the plow," it said. But another one scoffed at this idea. The land is only good for grazing and limited hay production on large spreads, it said. You will have to tell me what you think when we meet.

This is a terribly long letter, you will think that I am a chatterbox even though most people find me to be quiet. I will close now and get this to the post office so as to be sure that you get it next Thursday.

Sincerely yours,
Ellen Thomas

The letter came to Tom after a blistering day in the field. His oat crop had been pretty good—although very limited. He had only been able to break about three acres of sod early enough in the spring to plant small grain. He didn't own a binder yet, and his small patch wouldn't have been worth the expense even if he had the money to buy one, so he had cut the oats with the mower, and then tied it into bundles by hand and shocked them up as he went. He would stack the bundles later and use them this winter as feed, so he would not have to thresh. Some of his Norwegian neighbors were threshing now, and Tom longed for the camaraderie of the threshing crew.

Threshing was a social event for most farmers and their families, a time of community effort. A group of neighbors organized themselves into a threshing crew and went from farm to farm, often spending several days at each one. While at a farm, they were fed there, usually a big noon meal plus morning and afternoon lunch. The crew consisted of about a dozen men, and the farm wife often had extra help in the kitchen, too, so it made for a different atmosphere from the isolation in which most farm families lived and worked during the year.

Threshing was a time to work as a member of a team and a time to show off in front of the neighbors. Everybody bustled and put on limited airs. Horses were curried and shined, wagons and other gear were fixed up as they should have been in the first place. Ragged clothes were put aside; one kitchen vied with another for memorable meals. It was a time when the quality of your work, and the quality of your life, were open to inspection by the neighbors.

The judgments rendered were incisive, but usually kind and understanding. "There are things that Henry could learn about farming," somebody might say, "but that ain't really the problem. He already knows how to farm a damn sight better than the way he does it."

But for everybody, and especially for the younger people, threshing season was important because it was a time of social interaction, a time to live and work as part of a group. Each bundle pitcher had his pitchfork and his team of horses pulling a wagon-mounted rack. He would use the fork to load the bundles into the rack, stacking them carefully until the load towered high above his head. The men and boys would compete to bring in the biggest load from the field and could count on being complimented if they did. Tom still remembered the exact words of Carl Nelson, a man who farmed near the old home place in Minnesota. Tom had finished loading and had climbed up the standard on the front of the rack to take his place on top of the load. He had untied his lines, shouted "giddap" to the team, and started in toward the threshing machine from the far end of a forty-acre field of oat shocks, when he met Carl coming out empty. Carl had stopped and stared at him in admiration as he passed. "Goddamn, Tom," he said. "If you'd 'a stacked that any higher you'd have bumped your head up there."

The bundle pitchers would hurry to load and get back to the threshing machine early, so they could sit in the shade of a load by the cream can of drinking water and trade stories while waiting for their turn to pull up to the machine and pitch their bundles into the feeder. It was a time for pranks too—pranks that were more traditional than imaginative. The favorite was to sneak up to someone's load and tie one of his bundles to the floor or side of his rack, then laugh when he came to that bundle and strained to pick it up with his fork. Threshing had been that kind of a social experience for Tom in Minnesota, but only now was he beginning to realize how important it had been.

He had been a quiet and withdrawn member of those threshing crews. Tom "hoed his own row," it was said, but he fit in. That society was accepting of individualism in that respect; many of its members would be seen as a little odd by other standards.

Tom had been born into that group, and belonged, but now he was alone. He was beginning to realize that he lacked the ability to associate himself with a new group. He would be alone forever unless he found some way to get help, and it frightened him. Tom was only twenty-one—too young to be a hermit.

Following his usual Thursday evening routine, he hurried through his chores and started for the mailbox as the shadows began to lengthen. The dog went with him, a mongrel stray collie that had joined him in Gregory one day. Tom called him "Dog" after the custom of his father with the several farm dogs that had shared Tom's childhood. Dog wanted to help, and Tom had spent some time in trying to train him. Dog was patient and careful around the chickens, and assertive around the cow and her calf, so Tom thought he was lucky to have him. Dog mostly fed himself by catching gophers and mice and an occasional cottontail, although Tom did sometimes give him milk that had soured or other scraps from the table. Dog also ate ear corn from a small stock that Tom had bought for the chickens and chewed on horse manure if it was dry. He was also the recipient of the remains of whatever small game Tom could bag. Tom kept the shotgun and a twenty-two close at hand most of the time and frequently had pheasant, prairie chicken, or rabbit for meat.

The days were a little shorter now, but he would still be able to walk the six-mile round trip and be back by dark. The prairie had turned brown and tan, so the sparse grass crunched and crackled under Tom's resolute step. A large jackrabbit, brown for the season, bounded away across the prairie at their approach. Dog streaked off in pursuit, but the jackrabbits were always too fast for him. He came back panting and fell back into step behind Tom without a greeting. Dog was not demonstrative. Tom appreciated having him, but they had never become close like he and Gypsy were.

Tom hurried along, but the spring in his step that had propelled him along this route in June was strangely absent. Letters had become almost commonplace during the past two months, what with those that had come from Aunt Bess and the two priests, plus the two that had come from Ellen since that first one. His dream had rounded the corner from total fantasy to something that was at least remotely possible, and in doing so it had released a swarm of emotions. How could he ever go back from this if it failed now? But how could he ever cope with such an awesome responsibility if it became reality?

The mail-order-wife dream was one thing. She had fit into his deepest longings for love and companionship, but she was impersonal too, and took care of herself somehow. She was only there at certain times, and then went back to heaven or someplace. Certainly she did not huddle in dirty blankets on the earth floor of his two-by-four shack while the wind whistled through the cracks in the walls. And she did not shit in the straddle trench outside the front (and only) door, or in the straw shed with the cattle in the winter. He wasn't at all sure how girls handled problems of toilet, but he was sure that this wouldn't do. Wouldn't do at all. The thought of it opened up a whole Pandora's box of other things that wouldn't do, either. And he was helpless in the face of it all.

When the idea of a wife was only a dream he didn't have to worry about the family she was leaving, or how she would live from day to day until their magnificent farm became a reality, or how she could go to church on Sunday. Most of all, he didn't have to worry about what she would think of him—his moods, his actions that made him seem strange and remote to other people.

His whole picture of the future had come unhinged with Ellen's first short letter. The last rays of the setting sun that had seen him open the brown envelope on that June night had also seen the end of the mail-order-wife dream. What confronted him from the inside of the envelope was a real person. An honest, direct, infinitely sweet young girl who had a family that loved her. Tom was already in love by the time he rose from the grass and started the long walk back to the claim shanty, and the picture that came in the next letter cinched it. A girl in a white blouse with black hair drawn closely back from her face met his eye with a direct, honest, open gaze that captivated Tom—and frightened him. He felt sure that she had no concept of the destitute way in which he lived, and he felt guilty—as though he had misrepresented himself.

Dog bounded ahead as they neared the mailbox, and the old excitement gripped Tom again, but it was mixed with a presentiment of disaster. It seemed as if he had propelled himself over the crest of a figurative hill in a figurative toboggan, and now he was eagerly and fearfully hurtling down a mountainside in the dark.

Ellen's long letter was there. Alone on the prairie, in the red cast of the setting sun, he settled down into the brown grass and devoured its contents.

His answer was written by the light of his kerosene lamp as soon as he got back to the claim. It was short and matter-of-fact, partly because he didn't have much time. He had found out that old Palmer Benson's return route brought him along a trail five miles to the south of the claim at about ten o'clock on Friday morning. A family by the name of Dahl had a mailbox there, so Tom planned to hike down there early the next morning to post his answer in the Dahl's box. He explained this to account for the brevity of his note and said that he would call for Ellen at the Cody Hotel in Gregory in the early evening on Tuesday, August 23. "I am excited too," he added.

Tore

The dry August winds came from Montana, but they seemed to come from hell itself. They sucked the juice from every living thing—from grass, from tree, from horse, from man. The grass here knew what to do. Its life withdrew into its roots and went dormant, ready to spring back another time. The trees also were smart: they only grew in a few low areas where they could sink their roots into subterranean sources of water that could sustain them if they wilted their leaves. Tom was fortunate to have one such small area. With a sledgehammer, he had driven a sand point down about ten feet and attached a hand pump. So far, it had been reliable, although pumping enough water each day for the horses and the cow was hard work. The pothole that had supplied the animals with water was dry now.

Foreign plants, like corn, didn't have the defense mechanisms of native grass. Tom's sod corn needed several weeks yet. If this kept up without rain it would destroy the crop. Sunday was hotter still, and the wind kept blowing. He had started to cut a few stalks of corn each day for the cow. Without grain, her milk flowed better if she had something green, and the corn might fail anyway.

Fortunately, before the ground became dry and hard, he had dug the holes and set the tree trunk poles in place for his prairie hay shed barn. He worked on it for an hour or two most days. It was about ten by twenty feet with twelve upright poles cut from forked trees. He had set the poles so that the forks were about seven feet above the ground. The forks held cross poles that supported shorter sticks and brush to form the top, and he had covered that with prairie hay. The walls were formed of woven fence wire stapled to the upright poles, with a four-foot gap in the south side for a door.

Tom had also found a place along the creek bed where slough grass and reeds grew. Ordinarily, this was an area of water or mud, but the dry weather had changed that. It wasn't on his land, but the stuff was useless as feed, so he felt free to go in there, mow it, and haul it home. With his pitchfork, he kept piling this material over and against the walls of his barn. A covering of snow would complete the job when winter came. It looked ratty, a pile of junk hay with tree branches sticking out of it, but it would provide a lot of shelter.

When Tom turned from the desolate prospects surrounding him, his eye fell on something equally desolate but more urgent—the house, if it could be called that. He had to do something about the house before she came.

He tried to stand back and look at it analytically. Well, the roof was pretty good; he could say that. He had hauled out ten bundles of cedar shingles and a stovepipe feed-through from Gregory. And he had a pretty good door and one window, both on the south side. The walls were bad; you could see through them in places. "Dakota brick" (sod) houses were better in that respect. His plan had been to cover these weathered board walls with tar paper and cedar siding, and then to paint the building white, as his neighbors had done with their larger houses. Something would have to be done before winter, but he did not have money for siding and paint, or time now to do the work. He could pile prairie hay around the outside, as he had done for the barn, and snow was good insulation.

The inside was worse. The room was eight by ten feet, and its only furnishings were the stove, a table, a chair, and a stool. A six-foot board nailed to one wall served as a shelf; it held a conglomeration of items, and others hung from nails driven into the exposed joists. His dirty blankets occupied the dirt floor at one end of the room; the rest of the floor space was cluttered full to overflowing with piles of stuff, mostly farm related. There were feed sacks and harness parts, tools and a salt block, mower sickle sections, and a pitchfork with a broken handle. Tom's few clothes hung on one nail; a pail of axle grease on another. The shotgun was propped in a corner. There was a bucket of water with a dipper in it on the floor, and a wash basin on the table, plus the broken half of an old mirror on the shelf.

"This has to go," he decided. He spent all of Sunday afternoon hauling things out to the barn and straightening out what remained. He found a lot to throw away, including bones and rotten potatoes, and he hauled water and washed his clothes, and even his blankets. When he finished he surveyed the result; it looked worse, if anything. Amidst the squalor there had been a certain homeyness; now it looked like a pitiful nothing. He took the shovel and dug a new slit trench behind the barn, then filled the other one in and smoothed it off. That did look a little better, but it brought back the question, how can this work for her? He left his shovel there and wandered aimlessly off, eyes on the ground and thoughts moving from one crisis to another. As he moved along, he came upon Gypsy, tethered in the dry grass. He threw his arms around her neck, buried his face in her mane, and sobbed.

Finally, he was able to think again. His mind went at once to Ellen's letter and Aunt Bess's idea that he should sell and move back to Minnesota. He immediately thought of Tore.

Tore was the hired man back in Minnesota. In a larger sense, Tore was all of the hired men who labored and lived on the farms of America, the hired men who were to be written about by so many authors. Tore was the Silas of Robert Frost and the Victor Jensen of William Maxwell.

Tore had no life except the hay he pitched or the cows he milked, day after day, for someone else. Once a month he went into town and drank himself into such a stupor that he had to be hauled home a day or two later to dry out and start again. Tore was more a creature of the barn than of the house, as much another beast of burden as a man. Some farmers treated their Tore kindly, others did not. Usually, those who treated him kindly also treated their horses and cows well.

Tore was of a grizzled, indeterminate age—scarred, bent, and inarticulate. He became a Tore after being a child and remained a Tore until he died. By then, no one knew where he had come from.

The economic reality was that Tom would become a Tore if he went back to Minnesota. He knew that, except that he didn't think that the release of alcohol would be there for him. When he tried to picture Tore without his pitiful monthly drunk he could picture only an explosion—a murder, a suicide, an arson, or some nameless disaster.

And certainly, no Tore had a wife. Aunt Bess should know all of this, but the years had inured Aunt Bess to the Tores that surrounded her. She didn't really acknowledge them as fellow human beings.

These thoughts sent Tom back to the cabin with new resolve. He had to do something. Other houses had curtains, he thought, and rugs and wallpaper. He didn't know much about it, especially when faced with a dirt floor and walls with exposed two-by-four studs, but he decided to try. The farming would have to wait a day. Dawn on Monday saw him headed for Gregory with the team and wagon. The sun was low in the west by the time they got back, and urgent work with cattle, fencing, hay, and corn consumed the next three days, so Friday had arrived before he could turn to the home improvement project. Only two days remained until Ellen would board the train in Chicago. The world was rushing past like a freight train.

He carried everything out of the cabin, and swept out the debris that cluttered the floor. The rug and curtain should wait until last, he thought. He had wallpaper and stuff to make paste with; his idea was to fit the paper between the studs. The paper was too wide, and he did not have much luck trying to cut it, so he decided to fold it instead, and let it extend part way out alongside the stud. The dry boards pulled the water out of the paste, so he wet them down first. The paste worked better then, and the paper stuck pretty good. It took all day, and he ran out of paper before he finished, but it did give the interior of the cabin a strange new appearance. On Saturday, he tried to make some sense out of the curtain, and unrolled the rag rug over a part of the floor. When he had carried everything back in and put it away better, he looked around. Well, there it is, he thought. He was beginning to move like an automaton. It seemed as if his fate was out of his hands, as if he was moving along toward some prearranged destiny. Tore had often acted that way.

On Tuesday morning he did his morning chores, and then shaved and gave himself a bath. He had already curried the horses carefully and had them harnessed. At 9:30 they set out on the four-hour trip to Gregory. The weather had changed; the incessant arid wind was gone. It was hot, oppressive, muggy. Dog followed along behind the wagon. They went directly to the livery stable when they got to Gregory. Tom unhitched the team and put them up, and was assigned a sleeping bunk for himself. "We'll be leaving about four in the morning," he told the man in charge.

"I'll keep hay in front of them, and there's oats in the barrel if you want to feed them again before you start," the man said. "The tank outside will be full, so you can water your team before you leave."

"OK," said Tom. The man stepped outside and then came back. "Looks like a storm comin'," he added.

Tom glanced at the roiling western sky, and then went to his bunk and sat down to wait until it was time to go to the hotel to meet Ellen. He was strangely calm.

Ellen watched Yankton disappear as her little train gathered speed again—modest speed, to be sure, but they were clipping across the prairie now. The route had turned away from the Missouri River for the first time since they left Sioux City. The scene outside the window had changed to a vast reach of blue sky and brown, wind-blown grass, dotted by occasional farmhouses and green fields of corn in the distance. I'm really in Dakota now, she thought.

The train carried only one passenger car, and it was almost empty now. Most seats had been filled when they left Sioux City at 8:00 A.M., but those people got off at Vermillion, which was a university town. A group of four men had boarded at Yankton and were sitting together across from her. From their conversation she could tell they were headed for the state capital at Pierre and were connected with the government in some way. A man and wife whom she assumed were farmers had boarded in Sioux City and sat two seats behind her. They were dour, but nodded a greeting when Ellen smiled at them. The only other passenger now was an Indian man who had boarded at Yankton. He looked weather-beaten and wore what Ellen took to be the clothes of a working cowboy. He sat impassively in the last seat on the other side. It was hot and dusty in the train. Some windows were partly open to give a breeze; the breeze also carried a certain amount of smoke and cinder. Milwaukee seemed to be far behind her. Her father had been worried about her when he put her on the train in Chicago the night before, but she was excited and anxious to be off on this adventure. She still felt that way—minor physical discomforts had never bothered her.

The prairie did bother her, though, a little. Her imagination had not really prepared her for it. It reminded her of looking out over Lake Michigan. Soon she would not be just looking out, she would be out there. What had set her off on this strange journey? she wondered. How would it end? It was the most adventuresome thing she had ever done. As South Dakota glided past her window, Ellen fell to reviewing the past few months.

She *was* lonesome at home and at the brewery, that much was true. She had no beau, either. That was the nub of the matter, she had come to realize. She didn't want just any beau. She was more interested in being Ellen than she was in being somebody's wife. She *did* know that she wanted to be married. She had a maiden aunt, and Ellen knew Aunt Irma and her circle of friends, as well as some other old maids and girls older than herself who were becoming old maids. It was hard for them, Ellen knew—even those who had jobs. Many were teachers or had become nuns, and there were a few other office workers at the brewery. Some of these women had vital and rewarding professional lives—she knew teachers for whom this was certainly true. Her father knew a woman who was a secretary for Clarence Darrow, a well-known civil rights lawyer. But even those women were dissatisfied with their social lives, and many of them wanted to be mothers, too. Ellen had no urgent desire to be a mother—yet. That might come later, of course. She wanted to be married, but she wanted to retain her identity.

These ideas had only become clear in her mind since her correspondence with Tom had started. It had forced her to think, to come to know herself better. The ideas had been more like instincts before; now they were clearer. Her picture of pioneer women was that they were equal partners with their husbands—individuals in their own right. That was the appeal of this prospect.

Her vision of Tom was still somewhat neutral. Much of what she knew sounded good. He was a quiet and thoughtful person, physically strong, certainly daring—and he needed her, she could see that. But she didn't know him, and she knew nothing of farming. Both her father and Tom's Aunt Bess were full of doubt about his enterprise. She had no desire to marry a stranger to join him in economic disaster. This could not be a long courtship, she knew that. Even so, she was going to look carefully before deciding whether or not to leap. She was young, and the world had other places besides the Rosebud in Dakota.

The little train chugged along from stop to stop while Ellen mused. Then suddenly the conductor came in from the mail car and told her, "Platte next, ma'am." Minutes later, Ellen found herself standing alone on the station platform holding her small bag while the train chugged off down the track. "Dakota, here I am!" she exclaimed aloud to the nearly deserted Main Street that lay before her.

She could see the sign of the Frontier Hotel a scant block away, so she set off up the wooden sidewalk toward it. A chubby, affable lady in a red-and-yellow gingham dress greeted her when she stepped into the small lobby. "You must be Ellen Thomas."

"I am indeed," answered Ellen.

"I'm Mrs. Herther. My husband and I own the hotel," said the lady. "I have your letter here. You can call me Lillian."

Lillian was friendly and helpful and soon had Ellen settled in a room. Ellen asked about the mail wagon to Gregory. "Yes, I told Frank, as I said I would. He'll be by to pick you up at eight tomorrow morning," answered Lillian. "I'll send him word that you've actually arrived. The restaurant across the street is open at six if you want breakfast. It's about the only good place in town to eat. George and I usually have supper there. We'd be glad to have you join us if you'd like."

"Thank you, I would like that," answered Ellen.

"Fine, come down to the lobby about six-thirty, then."

Frank was as good as his word and pulled up to the hotel entrance at five minutes before 8:00 the next morning. Ellen was ready and waiting, and he helped her aboard. "Don't often get a passenger," he said, as he greeted her with a smile. "Looks like we've got a hot and muggy day. We may be glad we've got an enclosed wagon if it rains."

Ellen joined him on the seat. The back of the wagon contained several mail sacks and some freight, so Frank added Ellen's bag to the pile. "They're talking about replacing this rig with a truck," Frank told her, "but I don't look for it to happen soon with what we've got for roads. The ferry was flooded out for three weeks this spring."

The buckskin team trotted along smartly at first, but it was too hot to keep that up, and Frank slowed them to a walk. The ferry was waiting when they reached Snake Creek Landing, and the team pulled the high-wheeled light wagon onto the deck without hesitation. It was obvious that they had made this trip before. By noon they were across to the west bank, and had stopped at a way station there, where Frank left a mail sack and some items of freight. He also gave the team a chance to drink at the water tank, and gave each horse a small ration

of oats while they rested and he ate his own lunch. Ellen was too excited to eat, and it was too hot anyway. He asked her what brought her to
Gregory, but she avoided the question by saying that she was to meet
friends there. She did say that her friends were interested in farming
west of Gregory, and asked what he knew about the farms there. Frank
shook his head. "I've seen too much of this country to think farming
will ever work there," he said. "That was all cattle country a few years
ago, and will be again. Dry years will see to that."

There was a long uphill pull away from the river valley; then they
headed across more flat country toward Gregory. Frank began to cast
an anxious eye on the sky to the west. "I do believe there's a storm making up over there. I hope we get to Gregory before it hits. It's not always
too healthy out here with the wind and lightning. At least it may bring
a little rain, we sure need that."

They did make Gregory before the storm, but just barely. The wind
was gusting up the dusty street, and the sky was darkening fast as Frank
rushed Ellen off at the hotel and took off toward the livery stable at a
gallop. The sky went dark as Ellen was being shown to her room, then
a strong gust pattered large drops of rain against the window. As if on
that signal, a blinding flash of lightning lit the street outside. For an
instant the world stood in stark, brilliant contrast, then dark returned
and a deafening crash of thunder rattled the windows. Torrents of rain
and gale winds followed, while the lightning flashed and the thunder
roared. Gregory huddled under the onslaught.

Twenty minutes later it was over, and men were venturing out to
look at the damage. It was minor—one section of wooden sidewalk
had been carried away by the water and another was buried in mud.
The ramshackle roof from the little shed where Fred Kincaid stabled
his cow was gone, pieces scattered across the field south of the harness
shop, but the shed was empty and ready to fall down anyway. Within
another half hour, the sun was out, the water was receding into the
soil, and the temperature was in the seventies. A beautiful day. Ellen
stood in awe. It had been the most violent thing she had ever seen. It
had gone as fast as it had come, and it had taken with it the heat and
the dust and the misery. Suddenly, Dakota was a lamb.

She turned to get herself ready. Tom would be coming at 4:00.

Tracks in the Grass

At 3:50 Ellen went down to the lobby to wait. She sat in a comfortable chair facing the door and watched the few people who were around. At exactly 4:00 Tom came into the room. He recognized her immediately from the photo, and she could see the recognition in his face, so she stood up as he came toward her.

"Ellen?"

"Yes, and you must be Tom," she answered, briefly taking both of his hands in hers. "It's so good to see you."

"You look just like your picture, except that it doesn't nearly do you justice," he replied. It was true. The reality of her here exceeded his every expectation.

She laughed. "That was quite a welcome," she said. "Do you have some special arrangement with the weather god that lets you greet visitors with such a display?"

He smiled. "I was worried about you until the mail wagon came tearing into the livery barn. Frank told me that he had put you off here. I hope the storm didn't scare you."

"Oh, it did, it was the most violent thing. It was awesome, but I wouldn't have missed it for the world. Do such things happen often?"

"Not often enough, I guess," answered Tom. "The rain that came was a godsend compared to the little damage that was done. I'm glad you reached the hotel before it hit, though. Being out in a storm like that can be dangerous."

Ellen shuddered at the thought. "Are you going to show me Gregory now?"

He was pleased at the prospect. "There's not much to see," he said, "but we can look around. You've probably never been in a place like this before."

They spent the next two hours walking around Gregory—looking and talking. They toured through the Mercantile and looked at the post office. "This will all change quite a bit when the railroad gets here," Tom told her. "They're building a corral and an elevator, so they'll be able to ship cattle and grain out of here."

They even visited the livery barn so that Ellen could meet Gypsy and Buster and Dog. It had been a hard summer for Gypsy, and she was thin and bleached out compared to the beauty she had been in the spring. Even so, she was gentle and huge, and Ellen loved her at once.

She went into the stall and stroked Gypsy's muzzle. Dog resisted her charm, though, and slunk away at her approach.

Ellen wanted to return to the Mercantile, so they did and watched the farmers who were there as customers, stocking up on supplies. She became particularly interested in watching the women. Some of them were furtive and withdrawn; this disturbed Ellen. She had heard stories of pioneer women, stories of how the isolation of the bleak prairie had preyed on women's minds until they became deranged. But this was different, she knew that. Those stories were set in the Dakota that had existed thirty years earlier.

About 6:30 they returned to the hotel. Ellen went to her room for a few minutes, then she met Tom in the lobby, and they went to the restaurant for supper. Tom asked her about her father and her life in Milwaukee, and they talked of that briefly, but she wanted to start hearing about the farm. A girl at the brewery came from a farm near Milwaukee, and she had taken Ellen there one Saturday to give her an idea of what a farm was like. Tom said that he was afraid this wasn't much like that, but the conversation about the farm wasn't really very successful. She would have to look for herself. Since they were going to start so early they broke off the conversation at 8:00, and Ellen retired to her room. Tom would be at the hotel at 4:00 A.M. with the team and wagon.

It was not to be a night when either of them would sleep well. Tom was in hopeless torment. She was perfect! But he had nothing to offer. He could not bring himself to deceive such a girl, and even if he did it would only bring a worse disaster for both of them later. Well, tomorrow would take care of it. She would undoubtedly head back for Milwaukee after she saw his sorry claim. It would nearly kill him to see her go, but at least it would put this blunder behind him. His whole world focused down to tomorrow; there was nothing beyond tomorrow for Tom now.

Ellen was sleepless, too. What a strange, but lovable, young man. It almost seemed as if she was older than he was. The thought occurred to her that he was like the brother that she had always wanted. "Well! What nonsense are you talking?" she asked herself. "Your father would be aghast. You came out here to look at a farm and to meet a prospective husband. Have you forgotten that?" But she could not get her mind back on her mission. She slept fitfully and dreamed, and puzzled about Tom until the alarm clock jangled her awake at 3:30.

It was still dark when Tom came into the lobby to get her, but a hint of rose tinged the sky in the east. He helped her up to the spring seat, untied the team from the hitching post, and took his place beside her. Vega and Altair were brilliant above the black western horizon ahead as the wagon moved along the trail out of Gregory. Dog dashed about, happy to leave the confusing smells of town behind, then he took up a position to Buster's right front and trotted along in formation as a many-hued glow built up in the eastern sky behind them.

They talked quietly, as if fearful of disturbing the magnificence around them. "I got some coffee and sandwiches," Tom told her. "We'll stop after it gets light and warm it up for breakfast." They did that about 6:00, as the morning sun began to warm the prairie. Tom had wood for a small fire and a hook to suspend the coffee pot over it. They sat on the back of the wagon with the sandwiches and coffee between them and in front of them on the extended wagon reach. Ellen had never had a better breakfast, she said.

"Sometimes it's windy, and cold—or dusty," cautioned Tom. "Then it's not so good."

It was nearing 8:00, and they sat in peaceful silence as the team plodded along, when Ellen caught a glint of reflected sunlight from a spot ahead on the trail. "Look," she said, pointing. "There's something bright there."

"My mailbox," said Tom. "That's where your letters come to me. We're getting close to home now."

His remark brought Ellen back to reality. The ride had been idyllic, but she looked around with new eyes now. They had not seen a human since they left Gregory. The prairie stretched away in all directions. What must this be in the winter, she wondered. Or during the long droughts that everybody talked about. This trip had been a glorious experience, but could anyone imagine living here?

Gypsy and Buster nickered, and Dog dashed ahead as they pulled into the claim. Ellen was staring in disbelief. Could this really be the farm they had talked of? Tom watched her from the corner of his eye and could plainly see the reaction that she tried to hide. Actually, it looked better than it had when Tom left it the previous morning. It had rained here too, Tom saw with relief. The amazing grass was already turning green again, and there was no apparent damage from the wind, or any sign of hail that could have wiped out the corn crop. Tom pulled up to the barn, and the cow observed them from her tether nearby, while her calf frolicked around her. Tom and Ellen sat for a moment, each searching for a way to break the silence.

"Looks like the cow wants water," ventured Tom.

Ellen seized the conversational overture. "The calf is so lovely. How does its mother get water?"

Tom explained that he had to water the cow and the horses with a hand pump now, because the pothole had gone dry. "The team could probably use a drink too," he said. "We might just as well take them down there now, before I unhitch. I can show you some of the farm while we're at it." He realized that he was avoiding the moment when he had to show her the inside of the cabin. It looked tiny from the outside, and its bare wooden boards were unwelcome, boorish intruders against the quiet of the prairie. Tom felt now that his efforts at interior decorating had been utterly foolish and that he had only created a glaring, cheap incongruity. It had been bad when he started, but at least it had been honest. Now it looked like a pathetic, carnival fraud.

Ellen was enthusiastic about his suggestion. "Wait here a second then," he said. "I'll get the cow." He went to where she was tethered, pulled her stake from the ground, and led her over to the wagon. The calf spooked along behind as Tom made the rope fast to the back of the wagon and climbed back up on the seat beside Ellen. Gypsy and Buster set off across the field, with the cow and calf trailing behind.

On the way they passed the small field where Tom had harvested his oat crop, and he explained to her about that and about his intention to break more sod there this fall. The breaking plow was there and Ellen wanted to stop and have him explain breaking sod. He suggested that they do that on the way back—"I could take the team off the wagon and plow a couple of furrows to show you," he suggested. "Oh, good," she agreed.

This was much better. They watered the animals and had drinks of the water for themselves. Tom labored at the pump while Ellen made friends with the calf and the cow. Even Dog tolerated her better. Then they left the cow tethered near the pump, and drove over to the cornfield, where they dismounted again and walked through the field. Tom showed her how the developing ears were progressing, and they found a few that were beginning to dent. That led to a discussion of the miracle of growth and the rain of the night before. "What if it hadn't rained?" asked Ellen. Tom shrugged, "The corn would have died," he said. "What would the animals have eaten in the winter then?" she asked. "The animals may have died, too," he murmured.

After that, he said that he wanted to walk to the other end of the field to see if he might bag a pheasant there for their dinner, and suggested that she wait here near the wagon. He would be gone for ten minutes or so. Actually, this was partly a ploy to allow him to answer the call of nature, and to give her a chance to do the same, and she understood it to be such.

When he came back, they returned to the wagon and made a tour of the boundaries of the farm. Tom pointed out the houses of two neighbors that could be seen. During the ride he suddenly pulled the team to a stop and held up a hand for silence while reaching for the shotgun. Ellen's untrained eyes hadn't even seen the pheasant in the tall grass along the boundary. Gypsy and Buster barely flinched at the shot, and Dog raced to retrieve the bird. "Looks like pheasant for lunch," said Tom.

Tom also talked about his plans for the various parts of the farm — plans that he had not mentioned, even to himself, for many weeks. He became suddenly uncomfortable with such talk, though. It felt as if he was lying to Ellen. As if he had lied to himself for a long time until reality made him stop, and now he was lying to her. He fell silent and looked around at the prairie, and at the neighbor's house in the distance. Another picture of the future imposed itself. There were no cornfields in this picture. His neighbor's farm had swallowed his and many others, and had become a ranch. Most of the settlers had left, and Gregory had shrunk instead of growing.

Ellen sensed his mood and thoughts. "How about that sod-breaking demonstration," she asked.

It was well after noon by the time they got back to the cabin and barn. This couldn't be put off any longer, Tom realized. They would have to on their way back to Gregory by 4:00, and it was nearly 1:00 already. "The horses should have a little time out of the harness before we have to start back to Gregory," he told Ellen. "We'll have to remember to water them again before we leave too." She watched while he unhitched, then held the lead ropes while Tom pulled off the harnesses and draped them over the sides of the wagon. Each horse got a ration of oats and was tethered in the grass; then Tom plucked and gutted the pheasant on the wagon end gate and stopped at the garden patch to pull a few carrots.

"I'm afraid the house isn't much to look at," he finally brought himself to say. "I tried to fix it up a little before you came, but I only made it worse."

"Stop fretting about it," said Ellen. "Let's go there and cook this pheasant."

The inside of the house turned out to be worse than either of them had expected it to be. The driving rain that had greeted Ellen in Gregory had come through the cracks and spaces in the board walls. The soaked wallpaper had given way to the wind coming through the cracks, and now lay in caked mud on the floor or hung in forlorn festoons everywhere. The floor was dry again now, but mud and water had inundated Tom's new rug. Only the curtain survived. He sank into the chair, near tears, and looked at her helplessly, begging understanding. "The storm," he said.

She went to the side of the chair and hugged his stooped shoulders from the back. "Of course, the storm," she said. "I saw the storm. For heaven's sake, please don't fret so. You should never have tried to do this for me in the first place."

She wiped a tear from her own eye as they remained there like that for a moment. Then he rose. "I know," he said. "I knew it couldn't work, but I kept doing it anyway. I didn't know what else to do." He looked around and smiled ruefully.

"Well, who's going to cook, you or me?" she asked cheerfully. Tom decided that he should do it because his kitchen wasn't really equipped very well. Ellen said that she didn't know if she could stand to watch a man cook for her and that she wanted a chance to explore around outside by herself a little anyway. He should call her when dinner was ready. They dropped back into a mood of pleasant camaraderie that lasted through the afternoon and until they were on the way back to Gregory.

Tom headed east from the farm on the return trip, instead of north toward the mailbox. This route was a little shorter, but rougher. They came out on the main trail about ten miles west of Gregory as the shadows began to lengthen.

"We should talk now," Ellen said. "It may be hard to find a good time later. The mail wagon will pick me up at the hotel early tomorrow morning, and I'll get the Sioux City train in Platte tomorrow afternoon. Frank said to be ready by five, so you and I won't see each other tomorrow. Will you stay at the livery stable again tonight?"

"No. As long as I won't see you in the morning anyway, I'll probably go back to the farm tonight," he answered. "There'll be a big moon until well after midnight, so it will be a good time to travel."

They rode in silence for another half mile before Ellen spoke again. "I feel as if I've always known you," she said, "and I feel as if you can probably read my mind, but I want to tell you what my thoughts are anyway, to be sure. I think you already know that I could never do this; it is so remote and strange, a different world from Milwaukee."

"Yes," said Tom. "I felt sure of that, and I didn't want to try to convince you otherwise. It might cause you to be hurt—it probably would, and I couldn't stand to be the cause of that." They rode on in silence again.

"I have to say something else too," Ellen finally said, "about us personally. Almost as soon as we met I started to feel as if you were my brother—the brother that I never had. That feeling has deepened, and now you have become my very dear brother. I know it's inappropriate, but I can't help it. I know I should be looking for a husband, but I'm not really even interested in it right now. I hope that I will be later, but it won't be you. You will always be my brother, whether I ever have a husband or not. Meeting you has been the greatest experience of my life." Tears coursed down her cheeks. Tom put his arm around her shoulders and hugged her to his side. He said nothing. He had sometimes longed for a sister too, but he would never think of Ellen as a sister.

After a bit, she pulled herself away and wiped her face and blew her nose. Then she faced him on the seat. "And there's a third thing. You haven't told me what you think of your Aunt Bess's idea that you should come back to Minnesota—or what you think of the future of farming here, or how you can live in such a lonely place." Tom knew he had to give some kind of an answer this time, even if he had to lie a little.

"No one knows what the future will be here," he said. "As to Minnesota, Aunt Bess hasn't really given you a true picture. I can't go back there."

They rode on and came into Gregory as the sun reddened for its fall into night. Tom put the team into the livery barn, and he and Ellen went to the restaurant for supper. It was nearly dark when they walked back to the hotel. "Let's say good-bye here," she said, stopping on the side porch by the railing. She hugged him and cried again, and laughed, against his chest. He held her in his arms for a moment, then she stepped back and took his hands, as she had done when they first met. "I'll write when I get home so you'll know," she said. "Have a good trip back in the moonlight. Good-bye, and thank you for a wonderful day." She watched as he walked down the street toward the stable.

The next day was Thursday, and Tom rose early. He had reached a decision during his moonlight ride home last night, and he wanted to get to the mailbox before Palmer came around on his route. Ellen was already on her way to Platte, he reflected after milking the cow and boiling his morning coffee. That was good.

He cleaned the wallpaper out of the cabin and set it to rights, taking a last look around the room before he closed the door.

His next actions were strange. He first went to the cow and took the collar from around her neck, allowing her to roam free. She and the calf set off to investigate a herd of cattle on a neighboring farm in the distance. Then he did the same thing with Gypsy and Buster. They stood there, puzzled by this unaccustomed freedom. Tears came to Tom's eyes, and he hugged Gypsy's neck. "You've been so wonderful, someone will be lucky to have you," he said into her mane. Then he took his shotgun, and he and Dog set off up the trail to the north.

Later that morning, Palmer Benson came briskly along the trail toward Tom's mailbox. He had no letter for Tom, but the flag on the box was up, indicating there was a letter for him to pick up. Suddenly, he jerked the team to a startled stop and leapt down from his seat. A moment's investigation showed him that he did have something to pick up, but it was not a letter.

The mail came this way every Thursday. Usually.

But today was not to be usual for the mailboxes farther west on this route. Palmer Benson made a loop to turn around, and headed his mail wagon back toward Gregory. Beside the mailbags in the back of the wagon lay Tom Fleming's body—and his shotgun with an empty shell in the chamber.

Dog crouched beneath the mailbox and sniffed the blood-soaked ground in bewilderment.

DAVID'S
DRUMMER

The Brethren

Dignity. The word raced in circles within Joel's brain. His father had
taught him the word just for today—just for this important meal.

He was twelve, and this was to be his first meal with the men. Using
the basin under the cottonwood tree, Joel washed his face and hands
clean from the soil and sweat of the bean field. Then, holding his
black hat in his hand, he filed into the dining hall behind David
Hofer. Father was already seated at the main table with Mr. Decker,
the steward, and several other men. Their black hats hung from pegs
on the wall behind them. The serving table at the other end of the
room held large pots and pans, and the aroma of chicken and
dumplings wafted across the room to Joel's appreciative nose. His
mother and two younger girls stood by the serving table, waiting. The
shadow of a conspiratorial grin passed over his mother's face as she
caught Joel's eye.

For a moment he longed to be at the children's table with Mama,
but he knew she was proud to see him here, and he was proud too.
The line moved on, and he found his place, hung his hat, and sat.

Mr. Decker opened the meal with an announcement; he spoke in
an old German dialect that was evidence of the sect's long exile in
Russia, far from its German origins. Today, June 13, 1918, was an
anniversary. This Gadsden, South Dakota, Hutterite commune of one

hundred souls was ten years old. "Our *Brüderhof* has prospered. We thank God for that, and pray that he may deliver us from our present dangers," the husky man added. Then he nodded toward one of the elders, who rose to offer grace. Nothing was said about Joel.

On a rainy morning a few days later, Joel was free from the work in the field and was tagging around after David. David would soon be twenty-one and was at the center of one of those dangers. A great war was on. David would have to register for the draft on his birthday, and the Hutterites were conscientious objectors.

"Hold the sack a little higher, Joel," said David as he braced to keep corn from spilling to the ground. They were at the roofed corn-crib east of the colony house, shelling ear corn with the hand sheller. It had a large crank that David could turn with one hand while feeding the husked ears into the iron cone on top of the machine with the other. The shelled corn came out of a chute on the bottom and into a bushel basket. The bare cobs came out the back and accumulated in a pile. Joel would later carry the cobs to the kitchen to fuel the cookstoves.

When the basket was full of shelled corn it had to be emptied into a sack. The filled and tied sacks piled nearby showed that David had been on the job since early morning. Emptying the basket into the sack alone without spilling any of the precious grain was difficult, so David was glad to have his young friend there to help.

"Have you seen Greta Kleinsasser yet?" asked Joel with a mischievous grin. Greta had recently come from the parent Bon Homme colony to help in the kitchen. Her arrival had sparked a lot of interest, partly because of her jolly good humor and partly because of her bulk.

"Well, yes, I guess I have," said David, responding with mock seriousness. "Or at least I saw part of her through the kitchen window."

"How about Annie Entz? Did you see her too?" Joel was teasing now and knew he had hit his mark when David's neck reddened. David and Annie were in the early stages of a Hutterite courtship. He liked her very much, but he had trouble expressing his feelings to her or to the community.

"They were looking for a boy about your age to work for the German schoolteacher," David finally replied. "Maybe I should suggest you for the job, since you've got so much to say."

Joel made a face. "I was just foolin' around," he said. "I like Annie too."

David smiled; banter like this was fun. He felt uninhibited with Joel, but reality was always close at hand. David would never be carried away with romantic ideas. Both he and Annie were old enough and nearly ready for the real entry to adult life—baptism. They were of the Brethren and would accept the decision of the colony about marriage without question. They were here to glorify God, not to enjoy themselves. If life brought hardship or trouble, that was to be expected. Reward would come in the afterworld, not here. Life was like a job—the idea was to do it well and get it over with.

That evening, after the church service and supper, the men gathered on the porch as usual. The clouds had evaporated in the warm afternoon sun, and lengthening shadows spoke of rest from another hard day of work. Five acres of alfalfa, freshly cut after the rain, filled the air with a perfume that would fetch a king's ransom in New York. Meadowlarks trilled their mating song from the horse pasture across the trail, and a gopher whistled indignantly as sheep grazed through his green domain.

Pipes were filled from a large community can of Prince Albert and studiously packed as each man took his accustomed place. Some sat on benches using the porch rail as a footrest; others preferred to loll on the floor with back and shoulders propped against a post or wall. It was time for talk, and Joel loved to listen. As usual, he was the only child there. The others were already behind the English school organizing the nightly game of "Kick the Can." Joel didn't like to miss the game, but this was irresistible.

As the Hutterite men gathered on the porch to talk, a parallel event was taking place in Gadsden. It was the second Wednesday, the regular night of the community club picnic, and the citizens of Gadsden had also gathered to talk. As it often did, their talk eventually turned to their Hutterite neighbors.

Tim Timmerman was there, even though he preferred to hold forth in the saloon or the barbershop, where there were no women to contradict him.

"Hello, Tim," said a farmer he knew slightly. "I see by the paper you're a big shot now. Head of the War Bond Committee."

"No, not a big shot. Just trying to help," said Tim, looking modest and noble. "Our boys suffered terrible casualties during the German spring offensive, especially at Château-Thierry, and we've got to get behind them one hundred percent."

"We're in it full bore now, all right," said another man. "The French and the British have been dying like flies over there for years, and now it's our turn. Millions of men there in the mud and cold in trenches with barbed wire and poison gas. It practically rains gunfire and cannon shells. The *Argus Leader* had an article—said Allied factories have produced nearly three hundred million artillery shells for this war."

"Yeah, I saw that. Nine billion rounds of rifle and machine gun ammunition too. Hard to even imagine."

"Well, it takes nine billion stacks of greenbacks too," said Timmerman. "That's why our committee decided to put quotas on everybody. It lets people know what's expected of them."

The wife of the depot agent chimed in. She didn't know much about war bonds, but she knew Timmerman well enough to be uncomfortable with this idea. "Seems to me you're playing God with other people's money," she said. "Can you enforce these quotas of yours?"

"Patriotism will furnish all the enforcement we need as long as everybody knows that everybody else is puttin' in their share. If there's any slackers, we'll put the pressure on 'em, and they'll come around," he answered, staring pointedly at her.

"How about them Hutterites out there, Tim?" asked another man. "They've got money, but I heard tell they won't buy a nickel's worth of bonds. They say war's against their religion. That's why they came here in the first place. I heard that the Germans killed most of them and chased the rest out over this same argument three hundred years ago."

"Well, sounds as if they've stuck by their ideas for a long time and through a lot of suffering," said another. "I suppose they deserve some credit for that."

"Credit, hell!" exploded Timmerman. "They live here and get the advantage of it like everybody else. They've done damn well out there, but now that the country is in a pinch they don't want to help. They refuse to salute the flag or wear a uniform, and now you say the bastards are going to even refuse to loan the country money at a good rate of interest to buy equipment for the soldiers that are dying for them. They're the next thing to traitors as far as I'm concerned. You can damn well bet we put a quota on them, and there's going to be hell to pay if they don't fork over the money."

"Where did they come from in the first place?" asked another woman. "How do we happen to have them here? Are we the only ones with this problem?"

All eyes turned to Ann Smith, Gadsden's "old maid" schoolteacher. Ann was an institution in town—you could depend on what she said.

"Actually, almost all of the Hutterites do live in South Dakota," she said. "I think there are fourteen colonies here, plus two in Montana. They homesteaded here in 1874, so they are old settlers. They are good farmers and the colonies have prospered and grown. They live simply, but everyone has enough. The very young and the very old are as secure as the worker. No one is alone or isolated. They have no walls or police, and crime is almost unknown—there has never been a murder in a Hutterite colony."

"That's all fine, but it don't give them no right to welsh on their duty to the country," stormed Timmerman.

"I didn't say that it did, Mr. Timmerman," snapped Ann. He had once been her pupil, and he subsided now from force of habit.

"What bothers me about them is the way they treat their children," said another woman. "Those kids never laugh or have any fun at all. Except for the teachers, the adults totally ignore the kids and never talk to them or play with them. The kids go around like beggars, just craving adult attention."

"I don't like that either," said Ann, "and other colonies are even more strict than Gadsden in that respect."

Heads nodded and there was a murmur of agreement. "They certainly are strange," said the wife of the depot agent. "What on earth causes them to act that way?"

On the porch at the Hutterite colony, Six spoke first. His nickname referred to the fact that he was over six feet tall. Most people in the colony didn't even know his real name. Six was the sheep manager.

"I took the last load of wool into Gadsden to be shipped today," he said. "It was an experience I'll not soon forget."

"Why? What happened, Six?"

"Lots of things. It's the first time I've ever seen open hostility like that. There's a bunch of boys I often see. They're about sixteen or seventeen and don't seem to have anything to do but roam around town. They started to follow me and yell and make obscene gestures. 'Traitor,' they called me, and stuff like that. One of them kept yelling

'Draft-dodging Kraut bastard.' I had to kind of laugh at that, I'll be fifty next year.

"A little farther on I saw a woman I knew by sight. She sniffed and actually spat into the road. Then she turned her back on me with a big flounce."

"What did you do, Six?"

"Well, I just pretended to ignore them and went on about my business."

Jakela (Little Jake) sat on the porch floor with legs outstretched. He was a thoughtful man of normal stature and thirty-seven years; his nickname served to distinguish him from Big Jake, the dairy manager, who was said to be part grizzly bear. Little Jake stirred to rub his back against the post that supported it. "It's hard to imagine anything as big as that war," he said. "The men killed in just one battle outnumber all of the men in our entire brethren, and this has gone on for years. Imagine that all of the Hutterite men on earth were there and we were all killed in a single day. We would only be one drop in a big bucket. A few weeks later, no one would even remember anything about us being there."

"God would remember," answered Benjamin Alt-Vetter, "and he would be displeased. Wars are terrible, a sin against God and man. God has commanded us to refuse to take part, because that is the only effective way to fight against such a sin. It is tragic that the rest of the world does not follow God's teaching, and I grieve for the millions of victims and their families, but we can only control our own conduct."

"I agree," said the first preacher from his seat by the door. "Most of the victims of war are innocent except for the fact that they participate."

"But don't many civilians suffer and die too?" asked David. All eyes turned to him. David was not yet baptized, was not yet a member of the church, and was thus not yet considered to be an adult. It was somewhat presumptuous of him to enter into such a conversation, even with a question. But he was well thought of and faced military conscription, so his question was answered.

"Yes, indeed they do, but most of them also participate by supporting their country's war effort in the name of patriotism. Our people have always refused to participate. They became victims too, but they went to death with a good heart, knowing they had obeyed God. We may yet be called upon for such martyrdom in this horrible and senseless conflict. Our neighbors may come to torture or murder us. Pray that each of us remains steadfast and true to our principles in such an event."

"Amen," muttered several of the men, including Little Jake, but he had other thoughts too. He was trying to understand the woman who had scorned Six, and others like her. Such hate was an emotion foreign to him.

"That woman in town," he asked. "What would cause her to hate Six? Do you suppose she has lost a son in the war, or something like that?"

"Not likely," suggested Mr. Decker. "Gadsden is a small place, and she is local. In a case like that, we would probably know of it."

Benjamin Alt-Vetter leaned forward to speak again. "Alt-Vetter" has the nature of an honorary title—wise old man. Benjamin had a tendency to speak in sermons, but his remarks were generally treated with respect.

"Hysteria," he said. "Hysteria is about the best word we have for such conduct, although it isn't really adequate. Civilized behavior doesn't come naturally to people—it is only a thin veneer. Beneath that, without God's continual guidance, they are like a flock of chickens that peck the odd-colored bird to death. They wait for any excuse to throw off the constraints of civilization. When our founder was burned at the stake three hundred and eighty-two years ago, mobs of people who didn't even know of him were there to cheer. Public hangings in England were public celebrations. Negro lynchings are festive occasions in this country. When the Bohemian churchman, Jan Hus, was burned for his ideas in Switzerland in 1415, an observer noticed a timid-looking little old lady in gray who hobbled piously forward to add her faggot to the pile. What Six saw is normal when conditions allow it. War hysteria translates into huge profits for powerful people, and those people are fanning these flames to give themselves more power over the labor unions. 'Patriotic terrorism' they call it. This won't end soon."

A long quiet period followed. One by one, faces grew hard and jaws set. Preacher finally broke the silence.

"Benjamin speaks well," he said. "We must be strong."

The next day was Wednesday. The sun rose in brilliant splendor over the cottonwoods along the creek, and Annie greeted it with all of the joy she would lavish on a dearest friend. It was wonderful to be in the world for a dawn like this.

Annie was tall for a girl—slender and strong. Her hair was jet black under a polka-dotted blue scarf that struggled to contain it. She always seemed to be smiling, even when she wasn't. This had caused her some problems when she was younger. Smiles are not appropriate for every occasion in Hutterite society, especially from children.

This morning she was doing her favorite job—bringing the cows in from the pasture for the morning milking. It was a child's job, and she knew she would soon lose it, but the morning was too immediate to dwell on that. She loved this time alone, even in bad weather, and today it was priceless.

She found the cows in the far end of the pasture, near to where the railroad tracks crossed the creek, just before sunup. They were a good half mile from the end of the lane that led to the milking barn, and that lane was another half mile long, so she knew there was no time to waste.

"Come, you sleepyheads," she called out, laughing as she roused them from the grass with her little switch. "On your feet. Big Jake will be ever so annoyed with us if we are late."

Getting the herd started toward the barn in the morning was, she told David, like moving chairs. Each cow moved forward only when she chased it and stopped as soon as she turned her attention to another cow. Annie rushed back and forth across the width of the herd, trying to assemble them together and move them forward. Gradually her charges changed from individual sleepy cows to a unit, a herd that moved together. We are like them in that, thought Annie—and it's often good that we are.

By the time she reached the lane, the sun was on the horizon. Its light, filtered through the tops of the cottonwoods, cast the peculiar, crescent-shaped, red-bordered shadows that Annie loved. Conditions had to be just right, and you had to be there at just the right time to see them. In another five minutes, they would be gone. The east side of each black fence post was covered with green grasshoppers stirring to life under the red rays of the rising sun. In a few more minutes, they would be gone too, and she was the only one who had even seen them. Only the cows had shared the sight, and she didn't think that cows noticed grasshoppers.

"Do the grasshoppers know enough to gather on the east side when they alight there in the evening?" she wondered. "Or have they moved there earlier this morning in response to the dawn? I must remember to look at these posts earlier tomorrow. Perhaps I can find out what those creatures are really up to."

Annie worked in the laundry during the day, and Joel talked with her when he brought in a bundle of wash from his mother. She told him about the shadows and the grasshoppers. "Is it true that you are going to stop bringing the cows in in the morning?" he asked her.

"I suppose so," she answered. "I like to do it, but I'm getting too old. Anyway, I'll be starting instruction for baptism soon, and there won't be any time for it after that."

"Can I have your job then?"

She laughed. "You know I'm not the one to decide."

"Yes, but they would probably take me if you suggested it. Maybe I could come with you for a few days. That way I'd be experienced, and I'd like to go with you anyway to see the things you tell me about."

"Fine," she said. "Tell your parents and meet me at the head of the lane at four-thirty tomorrow morning."

After supper, Joel saw David and told him about the arrangement. "That's good," he said. "I just found out that Annie and I and Katie Wipf are going to start baptism instruction at the end of this week, so you'll probably have the job sooner than you expected. Normally we would have to wait for the Lenten season next year, but the war situation is creating too much uncertainty."

"I'm happy for you," said Joel. "You seem very excited about the news."

"I am. For a Hutterite, except probably for dying and going to heaven, baptism is the most important thing that ever happens to him."

"How about marriage?"

"That's important too, but not as important as baptism. They'll be telling you a lot more about it in school soon."

Joel was happy, but he was also uneasy. His friends seemed to be moving away from him.

June rushed by. Days started early and ended late, in affinity with the sun. Joel liked bringing the cows up in the morning. Although he did not quite find Annie's lyrical exultation in nature, he did enjoy the early morning stint alone with the cows. He found pleasure in looking at the things she had pointed out for him. Except for her, he thought,

I would not have really noticed it so exactly.

A more immediate interest was the expansion of his world into the colony dairy operation. His willing and able hands soon made themselves welcome, and Big Jake, the taciturn giant, had a helper. Jake was a pioneer in the art of keeping dairy records. He didn't often explain the idea behind it very well to the other men, but Joel was curious enough to learn by watching. He became adept at getting the weight of each cow's output of milk tabulated properly, and took an interest in the operation of the ancient centrifuge that Jake had scrounged from the agriculture college in Brookings for measuring butterfat content of milk samples.

"That spotted roan has three daughters in the herd, and all three of them are producing in the top third of the herd," he mentioned to Jake one day as they waited for the cattle to file out of the barn.

"Noticed that, did ye?" responded Jake. Joel could see that he was pleased, even though he tried not to show it. Joel was delighted to receive such approval.

Trouble appeared on the Fourth of July. The day came on a Thursday during a busy season in the fields. Colony leaders knew it was a national holiday but had paid little attention.

That evening everyone was making their way toward the schoolhouse for the religious service normally held before supper. Some raucous shouting was heard, and they looked up to see a caravan approaching the colony from the direction of Gadsden. Decker recognized the first vehicle as belonging to the lumber company in Gadsden. It was a flatbed Reo truck with an open-air cab and hard rubber tires that jolted along over the rough road. The bed of the truck was filled with shouting men, and two large United States flags had been mounted from makeshift poles attached to either side of the cab. The truck moved slowly, keeping pace with a line of horse-drawn vehicles that followed. A pair of automobiles, one steered with a tiller, completed the parade.

As the caravan swung in off the road, it became apparent that many of the men were drunk and that all of them were hostile. Some waved bottles, others brandished clubs. The truck came on past the barns and the dining hall, and stopped before the congregation of Hutterites in front of the school. A man riding in the cab, evidently the group's spokesman, stood up and pulled some papers from his coat pocket as Preacher and Decker approached. The noise died down.

"We've come for your war bond money," shouted the man, brandishing his papers.

"And who are you?" asked Preacher, fixing him with a cold stare.

"I'm Timmerman, head of the War Bond Committee for this county," was the reply. "You know well enough who we are."

"Le'me take this club to the Kraut bastard, Tim," came a drunken voice from behind Timmerman. "He'll remember us well enough nexsht time."

Timmerman held up his hand. "S'posed to do this official," he said. Then he turned back to Preacher and Decker and waved his paper.

"The quota set here for you people is twenty thousand dollars, as you already damned well know," he said. "This here is your official notice. We intend to take the money back to town with us today."

"That's the way to tell the son of a bitch, Tim," someone shouted. "We ought to clean the bastards out right now."

"Yeah, what kind of shit is this anyway? Our kids are gettin' gassed and shot over there, and we let the enemy live right here in our own country."

"Yeah," answered many voices. There was an ominous murmur and snarl, with stamping feet and sticks and clubs beating on wagon boxes and the truck bed.

"Well, what's your answer?" demanded Timmerman, moving as if to descend from the truck.

"You have no authority here, or anywhere else for that matter," answered Preacher. "We have no money for you."

The crowd surged forward as Timmerman came down off the truck. Some had cans of gasoline and sticks with bundles of rags attached. They gathered around the truck behind Timmerman, who stood facing Preacher and Decker. "Let's burn 'em out," snarled one pimply-faced youth. Some seemed to agree; others seemed hesitant. A group of older men gathered around Timmerman for a conference. The mob of men waited restlessly, staring at the Hutterites. The Hutterites—men, women, and children—stood with stony faces and stared back. Joel pressed against his father's side and welcomed the strength of that sturdy body.

The impromptu conference ended, and Timmerman turned to his mob. "No fires this time, boys. We're supposed to give a week's worth of official notice, and we don't want trouble over that later. But bring up the spreaders. We'll leave a little salute to the Kaiser so they'll have something to remind them that we'll be back."

"The spreaders" were five large manure spreaders, each loaded with a ton of odoriferous chicken or hog dung and drawn by four big horses. Manure is used as fertilizer, and this wagonlike machine is used to spread it on farmland. It converts the dung into a spray of liquid and solid material that fans out into the air from the rear of the machine.

At Timmerman's signal the drivers wheeled their teams out of line and forward toward the school, where the machines were kicked into gear as the mob jeered. The teamsters swung their rigs expertly to the left as they passed the schoolhouse so that the rain of debris fell squarely upon the people and the building. The Hutterites stood their ground stoically as the stinking mess pelted them. A pebble struck Great-grandma Wipf below her left eyebrow, so a gush of tears and blood coursed through the dripping hog dung that covered her face. She collapsed to her knees from pain and clutched at the eye with both hands. But then, using her neighbor for support, she pulled herself back to her feet, lifted her now sightless eye to what she saw as heaven, and prayed.

The teams swung again to give the same treatment to the dining hall and to the long, low dwelling house where everyone lived. Then they spread the rest of their loads upon the foot path and, followed by the raucous crowd in wagons and cars, headed back toward town.

Silence reclaimed the scene, and the Hutterites filed into the simple schoolroom for evening worship. "We can clean ourselves later," said Preacher. "Our first response to any crisis should be prayer." At the close of the short service he announced that the evening meal would be postponed for an hour.

David went to the horse-watering tank, shook out his coat and brushed it and his trousers down with a broom. Then he drew a bucket of water and sloshed it over his face, neck and arms, scrubbing them clean. That done, he loaded a tub of water onto a cart and began to scrub down the entrance door to the dining hall. Others followed his lead. By bedtime, most evidence of the raid had already disappeared.

The next day, Joel and David were finishing up the cleaning job. The dung had been washed from the buildings and swept from the paths. They were raking it into the soil where the first rain would disperse it.

"It'll help our grass," said David, "so maybe they left us something good after all."

"I hope they don't expect thanks. I hear that Ankela Wipf will probably never see from that eye again." Joel fidgeted with his rake for a moment, then looked David in the eye. "Were you afraid?"

"I don't think so—not for myself at least. In baptism training we keep hearing that the best part of life will come after death, so why should I be afraid?" David had paused, and stood holding his rake and looking off over the prairie. He was talking to himself as much as to Joel. "In a way, I welcomed the danger. It was a test for me."

"I was afraid," confessed Joel. "I think I could have stood up to them and not cried or begged if they had come for me, but I was afraid."

"You're only twelve. At your age I would have been afraid too. It takes a while to understand. That's why they only baptize adults."

"Does Annie feel that way?"

"She does, in a way. We talked about it last night. Her ideas are more complicated than mine, but we agree generally."

"What else did you talk about?" Joel was suddenly back to his old light mischief, but this time David smiled.

"If you must know, little friend, we talked of marriage."

Joel impulsively threw his arms around David's waist. "Will it be soon?"

David held up his hand in caution. "We hope so, but there are complications."

"Well," Joel said, "I know you are almost finished with baptism instruction, and that the ceremony where you become members of the church is the Saturday and Sunday after next. What else is there to worry about?"

"My birthday is next Friday, and I will have to go into Gadsden on that day and register for the draft."

Joel's eyes grew large. "What will you do if you are drafted?"

"It's all worked out. If we are ordered to go, we will go, but after we get there we'll refuse to wear any military uniform or salute any flag or do anything against our religion."

"But what will they do then?"

"I don't know what they will do. I only know what I will do."

The World

On Friday, about midmorning, David washed his face and hands, put on a clean shirt, dusted off his hat, and headed toward Gadsden with a single horse and buggy. The draft board clerk was a lady who ran the office out of her kitchen. When David knocked, she came to the door immediately, dusting flour from her hands with her apron.

"I am David Hofer. I've come to register," he said.

"Yes, come in." She pushed the screen door open nervously.

His English was good, and he smiled and removed his hat as he came in. She seemed to be put at ease by his gesture, and offered him a chair. We may have our differences, but not all of the outsiders are like Timmerman's raiders, David decided.

Baptism was a solemn two-day affair. "Hutterites are not admitted to the adult world lightly," Preacher reminded the Brethren. It culminated on Sunday with the reading of the Taufreden—three sermons passed down from the sect's golden period in sixteenth-century Moravia.

The very next day, David and Annie talked with their parents and with Preacher about getting married. Annie was very forthright; she was a woman now. "If the war is to interfere with our lives, we want to face it together," she said. "We don't want to wait."

Preacher nodded. "The women of the colony seem to agree with you, and arrangements are simpler when both of you are from the same colony like this. I would suggest that three days would be enough. David, if you and your parents would make your formal calls on me and on Annie's parents Wednesday afternoon, we could have the engagement service that evening, and there would be three full days for the celebration before the wedding service on Sunday."

"You two sure are the center of attention around here lately," remarked Joel when he learned of the plan. "Two more church services with you up front!"

"Don't worry, there's a lot less ceremony to a wedding than there is to a baptism," David said, laughing, "and even less to an engagement. We'll be in and out of there in no time. Besides, there'll be four days of eating and drinking. Maybe we can fatten you up a little."

"The Allied counteroffensive in France was gaining momentum at a terrible cost to both sides," said the day-old Sioux Falls paper that was delivered to the colony with each day's mail. Five copies came and were passed from hand to hand. Almost all colony members had a good command of English, even though the old German dialect was their daily language.

German submarines were busy. The American cruiser *San Diego* and the steamship *Westover* went down with heavy losses, and three barges were sunk off Cape Cod by an audacious U-boat.

The "patriotic terrorism" practiced against labor unions earlier in the war was bearing full fruit; no one dared to even whisper against the war effort now. Hostility in Gadsden, and in other South Dakota towns, grew steadily worse. Newspaper editorials featured extreme positions, and front pages had pictures of children waving flags and tying bandages.

The Gadsden draft board was not to be caught napping or doing less than its share in such an atmosphere. Less than three weeks of married life had passed for David and Annie when the mail brought a notice ordering David to report for induction into the army.

Joel stopped by to visit David and Annie in their apartment that afternoon. He entered without knocking, as was the custom, and found Annie alone and crying. He had never seen such a thing before and went to her side awkwardly.

"What is it, Annie?"

She wiped her face and nose and handed him the letter. "Where is David?" he asked, after looking it over.

"He told me to stop crying, and went to tell Preacher about the notice," she answered. "He said it would be a disgrace for me to act like this in public. People would think I was not willing to accept God's way. He is right, of course. I must get myself under control. Please don't tell anyone that you saw me like this."

"I won't, Annie," he answered, and reached out to touch her shoulder. "Don't cry. You'll be all right. No one will get the best of David."

The following Tuesday, August 13, David boarded the train in Gadsden to report to the induction center in Sioux Falls. From there, his group would take the train to Fort Riley, Kansas, where they were to be sworn in and trained to be soldiers. Preacher, with his horse and buggy, took David to Gadsden to meet the train. He wanted these final hours alone to talk about David's mission. The colony watched their departure with grim foreboding.

An outdoor service preceded the departure. It was very formal; the Hutterites gathered with stony faces as if preparing for a siege. Annie stood in dignified silence with the rest; she and David had said their good-byes in their bed the night before.

"I love God, but I love you too," Annie told him. "I know that we expect our greatest happiness in heaven, but that seems impossible for me unless you are to be there with me."

"I know. I think it must be that we will be there together. Preacher would say that such a thought is too worldly, so I don't talk with him about it, but it must be. I couldn't face death for my religion so easily if I didn't believe that."

"I'll miss you terribly, tomorrow and every day and night after that. I want to tell you now because, after you go, there will be no one to tell. It would be a sign of weakness, and they would scorn me for it."

"Joel," said David. "If you do it in a mature way you can talk with Joel, and it will be good for him too."

"Yes," she said, hugging him, her eyes awash with tears. "I'm so glad that you like him, it says so much about you. It has been wonderful for me to share his friendship with you. The memory of that sharing will be even more precious now that we will have nothing else to share."

"We still have this night," he said, gathering her close.

Toward the end of August the Gadsden Hutterite colony became front-page news, thanks to Timmerman and his ardent "War Bond Committee." They were drunk with power, and some of them, often enough, with whiskey as well.

It started as a repeat of the previous raid as the colony gathered for evening service. The flatbed truck led the parade as before, but this time many of the raiders were masked and mounted on horseback. Preacher and Decker again moved forward to face Timmerman in the truck cab.

"We've come for our money," announced Timmerman.

"We have no money for you," answered Preacher.

"You have cattle. You have sheep. The slaughterhouse in Sioux Falls has money for them. Pay what you owe or we take it in livestock," thundered Timmerman.

"We owe nothing. You have no right here. Get off our land,"

answered Preacher, pointing to the road. His eyes blazed and his long hair streamed in the wind.

"Don't preach to me, you traitor Kraut son of a bitch," screamed Timmerman. "Go get 'em, boys."

His men dismounted and ran forward to form a line in front of the Hutterites. Many of them carried guns. Meanwhile, a dozen mounted men broke away from the group and galloped toward the barns and pasture.

The two disparate groups, vigilantes and Hutterites, stood facing each other across the dusty road. Here, on both sides, were the sons and daughters of Dakota pioneers. Preacher faced his people and held up his hands, shoulder high, palms outward—but the gesture was unnecessary. Even without the guns, no one here would have tried to use force to stop the angry men who confronted them. It was not their way.

The Brethren drifted together into small groups and stood in silence, staring with stony faces at the intruders. Their look bespoke contempt, and sorrow for mankind fallen so low. It was the look that the pious bestowed upon Roman soldiers gambling for the garments of Jesus.

The line of vigilantes wilted under the stare. Some looked down at their feet or adjusted their bandanna masks higher under their eyes. Listening to the bluster in town was one thing; this was quite another.

Timmerman rushed into the breach. "Stay your distance, and keep a sharp eye on 'em," he intoned like a Civil War general. "Don't give 'em an inch, and don't start feeling sorry for 'em. Jimmy Gleason gave his life and his mother is wandering up and down the road in shock. These scum are rich, and they won't even loan the government money at a good rate of interest to help. You're not taking anything from them. They'll get the bonds and redeem 'em later—after our boys drive that bastard Kaiser back into the North Sea."

"Goddamn right, Tim," responded a bearded man, raising his rifle over his head in a salute. "Our boys are dyin' for us over there."

The line stiffened and the impasse resumed amid a silence broken only by the distant shouts of horsemen and the bawling of cattle. Then the cattle appeared, shepherded by four riders. The horsemen steered the tame animals past the tableau outside the school and out on to the open road. Big Jake's experienced eye numbered the moving cattle at ninety-eight—steers, dry cows, and yearling calves.

Close behind the cattle, moving along with the colony's entire flock of a thousand sheep, came the other six horsemen. Two of them led, riding abreast. Each had his lasso on the same large ewe, constraining her to walk between them. Like sheep everywhere, the others followed in a close-packed, baa-ing mass, and the remaining four riders had little to do but tag along.

As the flock cleared the compound, the truck driver swung his rig about to follow. The gunmen backed away from the Hutterites to a safe distance, loaded aboard the truck and other vehicles, and followed the sheep down the road toward Gadsden and the railroad siding. Silence and dust descended together behind them.

The Hutterites resumed the church service and evening meal after checking on their gates, fences, and remaining livestock. Later, the men gathered on the porch to talk about what should be done. Joel was there to listen.

The council members said little in the early stages of the discussion. The elders wanted to see the topic explored. Colony decisions are reached through consensus.

Big Jake spoke first from his seat on the porch step. "Well, I'm glad they at least left the dairy herd. We don't have any immediate problem about food."

Six stared out across the alfalfa field toward the cottonwood grove as his thumb methodically packed the bowl of his pipe. "Yeah, you're right there. We're still in good shape for the rest of the summer if they leave us alone. The gardens are producing, and we have dairy products and poultry for meat."

"Sure, but then what? And will they leave us alone? In the long run, we can't make it if this keeps happening," said another man.

"I know. We depend on the rule of law as much or more than the outsiders do," answered Six, nodding slowly.

A vee of Canada geese passed over the cornfield and honked its way toward the setting sun. A girl from the kitchen brought a pail of beer, which was passed from hand to hand around the porch. David's father stretched his legs and scratched his back against a pole that supported the porch roof.

Little Jake finally broke the silence. "We have always supported the rule of law. We obey it and we pay our taxes. We support the government fully, except when it comes to war. If this country should refuse to tolerate our stand on war, then I suppose we would have to leave — try to find another place somewhere?"

"It has happened before, Jakela," said Decker. "We all know that."

"Yes, it has. But what happened tonight was not done by the government," suggested Six. "It is even possible that those men could be punished by the law for what they did, or that we could sue them in court."

"Timmerman would say they took nothing from us because we are to get bonds."

"Do you think we will actually get bonds and eventually get money for our animals?"

Silence fell again while they contemplated this possibility. Decker finally spoke.

"A lot depends on how the news of this raid is received by the general public. My guess is that many people will be critical of the raiders and that such a thing will seldom, if ever, be repeated. If so, it would not be enough to justify an exodus. We would lose a great deal by such an action—we have a large investment here."

"You may be right," said Benjamin, "but property may not be the important consideration. I have heard some very bad rumors about the treatment of young men from other colonies who were drafted into the army. If the stories are true, then we face a crisis because they were tortured. It has been centuries since Hutterites were physically tortured for their beliefs."

All eyes turned to Preacher, who had been listening from a chair at the end of the porch. He rose and came forward. "The rumors that Benjamin speaks of are of great concern, both to us and to the Mennonites. I have not spoken before for fear of spreading false alarms, but I attended a meeting of preachers in Menno today and was convinced that at least some of the rumors are true. A joint delegation has been sent to Washington to plead our cause with the secretary of war, and the Hutterites have also sent a delegation to Canada to look into their laws and the availability of land there.

"I agree with Mr. Decker that such a move would be very costly indeed, but even so, I don't think we could stay in a country that would torture our people for our beliefs."

"How about David?" said Little Jake. "Do we know anything about what has happened to him?"

"Not really," answered Preacher. "His wife had one letter, but it was mailed from Kansas City before his group was actually taken to Fort Riley for induction."

The conversation ended, and Joel went to talk with Annie. A chill had come over him when the men talked of torture and of David. The sight of armed men holding the whole colony at bay while others took away their livestock had affected him deeply. The colony, which had always been the center of power in his world, seemed small and puny compared to the outside forces that confronted it. His friend David no longer seemed invincible. Joel was frightened for David, and such fright as this was a new and terrible experience for him.

He was close to tears by the time he reached Annie's apartment. "Why, Joel," she said. "What has happened?"

"I am afraid for David."

She hugged his shoulders briefly, and then they sat across the table from each other in the gathering dusk. He looked toward her, pleading, aching for help. She fought against her own tears, shuddered, and tried to rise to the occasion. "I am afraid too, terribly afraid," she finally said. "I heard today that John Wipf of the Rockport colony was sent to the Alcatraz prison in chains and put in solitary confinement in a tiny cell in the dark. His clothes were taken and a military uniform was put beside him. He was told that he would either put on the uniform or die there, like the man before him did. The guards jeered at him and beat him with clubs. He was starved—given no food at all for four days. It was a filthy place full of biting and stinging bugs that caused his arms to swell up so bad that he couldn't get his clothes on when he was finally taken out of the cell."

"Did he put on the uniform?"

"No, he did not."

"How did you find out about this?"

"Greta heard about it when she went back to her home colony for her aunt's funeral yesterday."

They sat in silence for a few minutes. The world of Joel's childhood was disappearing into the mists.

"If David had been the one, instead of John Wipf, what would he have done, Annie?"

She sighed. "David marches to the beat of his own drummer," she said. "It's a drummer the rest of us can't always hear so clearly. I'm sure he would have done exactly as John did, except he would probably have lectured the guards for good measure."

Joel looked suddenly older. "He could be killed there."

"Yes, Joel. But David would say that any of us can die at any time.

The important thing is how we live."

Joel rose to go. "Thank you for talking with me, Annie. I don't know why, but I feel a little better now."

"I don't understand it either, but I think I feel better too."

The train with the Hutterite cattle and sheep arrived in Sioux Falls about the same time that the daily *Argus Leader* hit the streets with the story. The editorial page came out strongly on the side of Timmerman and his patriotic raiders. "If the Hutterites didn't like it," suggested the editor, "they should pack up whatever they can carry and go back to wherever they came from." Timmerman was in his glory. He invited reporters to join him at the slaughterhouse to cover the sale and photograph him with the check.

The president of the meatpacking company had a different reaction. After scanning the newspaper story, he hastily called for the company's lawyer.

When Timmerman and his jubilant crew appeared they were met by a stern-looking man in a black suit who passed out a prepared statement. His company refused to buy this livestock on the basis that its ownership was in question. Timmerman was ordered to get the animals off the company's property at once. Tim tried to climb onto a desk to make an inflammatory speech for the reporters, but two burly guards ushered him out the door.

By the next morning, the cattle and sheep were aboard another train, bound for Yankton, South Dakota, and an auction barn and corral there. Handbills were already being distributed in all nearby towns announcing a sale two days later. "TERMS—STRICTLY CASH," proclaimed the bills in large print.

Auction day dawned gray and rainy. Hundreds of people milled around in the mud that surrounded the outdoor sales ring, but most of them were spectators. Buyers were few, and as circumspect as church mice. Swarthy men swathed in slickers and Stetsons slouched in shadows and sent furtive signals to the auctioneer. When the hammer came down on each lot, a confederate of the bidder moved forward to the clerk to exchange greenbacks for a gate certificate, and anonymous riders appeared out of the mist to pick up the animals at the gate and disappear with them over some nearby hill.

Within an hour, the only remaining trace of the Hutterite cattle and sheep was the cash in Timmerman's hand—$14,882. It was a far cry from the $30,000 the animals were worth.

"Well, boys, it's not what we expected, but it'll still help. We'll put it in a trust fund in the bank here in Yankton until we can arrange for a ceremony to turn it over to the War Loan Board for bonds."

Tim, in his imagination, saw another front-page picture of himself on a flag-draped stage passing a check over to someone—perhaps a lovely girl—representing the board. But the board refused the money and the Hutterites eventually recovered the sale proceeds, although nothing more, after an inconclusive battle against anti-Hutterite measures in the legislature and in the courts.

The Conflict

David was an object of some curiosity but little hostility among his fellow inductees. His garb was standard Hutterite—black trousers, coat, and hat. The trousers were supported by suspenders over a colorful shirt, and David often carried his Bible in his hand. His letter to Annie was posted from Union Depot in Kansas City while his group waited for another train that would take them to Manhattan, Kansas; Fort Riley; and induction into the army. He told her about the routine of the past few days. "It may only be the calm before a storm," he suggested.

The storm started promptly upon their arrival at Fort Riley. Sergeant Schakel was assigned to be in charge of the group. He planted his burly body in front of David, and thrust his chin to within inches of David's face. "And what the hell are you?" he demanded.

"I am David Hofer."

"Maybe you *were* David Hofer wherever you came from, but you'll be *Private* Hofer here as soon as we get you out of that monkey suit and into a uniform."

"I will not wear a uniform. My religion forbids it."

"Well, kiss my ass," said Sergeant Schakel, stepping back from the rank in disgust. "You hear that, men? Private Hofer here says he's going to refuse to wear the uniform of the United States Army." With a sneer of contempt he stepped forward again, looming over David and jabbing a finger toward his face.

"I'll tell you this, Hofer," he snarled. "You've got another think comin' soon enough. You're in the army now. We got our own religion here, and it don't include takin' no shit from no greenhorn draftee. As far as you're concerned, I'M in charge here, and YOU do as I tell you. You belong to the army now. Is that understood?"

"I belong to God first," answered David.

Sergeant Schakel was grim. "Your heart and soul may belong to God, but I'll tell you this, Hofer, from this day forward, your *ass* belongs to me."

The army pretty much lumped the Hutterites in with the more numerous Mennonites, so David and three Mennonite men were assigned to Sergeant Schakel's care. David was the worst among the bad, because the Mennonite creed at least allowed them to do menial work. David refused to do anything useful.

There were seventeen thousand men at Fort Riley, and it only took a day or two before most of them knew of Sergeant Schakel and his strange small contingent of four men wearing black clothes and carrying Bibles. He made a great show of treating them with the utmost contempt, and others followed his lead. The "Hoots" were abused continuously.

The Hoots often marched along the streets of Fort Riley in single file with Sergeant Schakel barking and snarling at their flank. When they did, everyone they met stopped to jeer. If an infantry company marched past, its commander would always shout out, "ROUTE STEP —MARCH," leaving 150 men free to shout insults as they passed.

The Mennonite Hoots were Peter, Paul, and Samuel. The Brethren owed a debt of gratitude to the Mennonites that dated back to 1842 and the Ukraine, but David mistrusted his companions. Paul was their leader, and seemed to always search for compromise. Samuel was weak and whiny; David often upbraided him and reminded him of the insignificance of this life, compared to the glory of the hereafter for those who did the Lord's work in a responsible way.

Schakel housed his Hoots in a small room intended as a place to store coal. He made them clean it up and keep it spotless even though there were no bunks or furniture of any kind. The Hoots slept on the floor and were allowed access to the latrine and shower at certain very restricted times. They had to clean these to pass inspection after each use, even though they often found them dirty. In effect, Schakel had converted them into latrine orderlies. David was willing to do such work—it was simply providing for his own needs, not furthering the war effort.

Schakel also banned them from the mess hall, deeming them to be a contaminating influence. The Hoots were to prepare their own meals as best they could with rations they were to pick up at the back door of the mess hall at 5:00 A.M. daily. The cooks were unsympathetic and careless about what they put in the bucket for the Hoots, so David and his associates grew thin as September wore on.

One day Schakel had the Hoots unloading sacks of potatoes from a boxcar. As usual, Peter, Paul, and Samuel did the work while David stood defiantly by. It was hot, dusty work, and Samuel was hungry, tired, and upset. A group of drinking soldiers had invaded their room the night before and forced them into interminable "exercise" on the parade field, chasing them with motorcycles. After that, they were forced into cold showers with their clothes on, prolonged until Samuel was huddled into a corner of the shower stall, screaming and hysterical.

Today, David was berating him for cooperating with Schakel, and Samuel was desperately homesick. At that moment, Captain Gosset came walking by.

Captain Gosset had won a battlefield promotion in France. Most of his friends had been killed in an abortive defense of a meaningless knoll outside Château-Thierry, during the German spring offensive. Despite his own wounds, Gosset was struggling in the mud in a trench trying to help a bleeding and semiconscious Lieutenant Tom Flynn, his good friend. A German soldier leapt down into the trench and thrust his bayonet toward them. Instinctively, Gosset shielded himself with Flynn's body. The bayonet caught Flynn in the Adam's apple, and the point came clear through his neck to emerge almost in Gosset's face. The German stomped his boot into Flynn's chest, jerked his bayonet clear, and lunged for Gosset. Just then an artillery shell with poison gas slammed into the trench wall, killing the German and partly burying all three men.

Gosset was pulled from the mud an hour later, and his body survived. He was revered and held in awe at Fort Riley, but his ways were often strange.

For Samuel, Sergeant Schakel and his other tormentors were like bullies on the school playground. If he could get to the teacher, or some authority, and "tell on them," then the bullies would be chastised and everything would be all right. Samuel knew what a captain was, but this was the first one he had ever seen up close. This was his chance!

"Captain, sir," he whined, "this sergeant has been abusing us terribly. We don't have any beds, we don't get enough food, he insults us continually with blasphemous profanity, and he mistreats us physically."

Gosset looked at the figure before him with apparent concern. "Why, imagine that!" he said. "Could you be more specific? Did the sergeant kick you?"

"Well, no, he didn't actually kick me. But he made me—"

Samuel got no further. Gosset turned brusquely to Schakel. "Sergeant," he said, "if this man gives you any more trouble, kick him right in the ass."

"Yes, sir," responded Schakel with a snappy salute. Gosset turned coldly on his heel and stalked away.

The demoralized Mennonites cut a deal with Schakel shortly after the Gosset episode. They agreed to wear cooks' whites on and off duty, and to work in the mess halls as permanent KPs. Cooks' whites are not really a uniform, they reasoned. They would continue to live in the coal bin, but they could eat in the kitchens where they worked. Best of all, perhaps, their mailing privileges would be restored. They would finally be able to write home and get mail.

David was truly alone now, thin as a scarecrow, banished from the coal bin, and forced to sleep and eat outside. October was coming on, and the nights were getting damp and cold. He was issued a shelter half, like everybody else, but it takes two shelter halves to make a two-man pup tent. "Don't complain to me," said Schakel. "You're alone through your own doing."

After two weeks of this, Sergeant Schakel made one last effort to reason with David. "The colonel has had enough of this, Hofer. It's a wonder he didn't court-martial all four of you to begin with. He didn't, but now that it's just you, we can't afford the time to screw around with it anymore.

"Unless you put on the uniform and start taking orders, you're as good as on your way to the military prison at Fort Leavenworth. I've seen the place, and I don't wish it on any man. They collect the scum of the earth down there, on both sides of the bars."

Columbus Day found David, shackled to armed guards, aboard a train bound for Leavenworth. The elaborate general court-martial procedure had been a meaningless jumble to him. He was sick with fever and diarrhea, and weak. One good thing had come of it: as a prisoner, he had been allowed to write a heavily censored letter to Annie. It was his first letter since the hastily posted note from Kansas City an eternity ago. There had been no incoming mail either, because no one knew his address. Before the Hoots broke up, Paul promised to write to Annie on David's behalf, so she got two letters.

Physically, it would have been hard for anyone to recognize the shackled prisoner on the train as the buoyant young man who left Gadsden two months earlier. He sat huddled on the seat, ragged and thin. The gaze of his sunken eyes was inward; he took little notice of what was going on around him, and his skin was gray despite an underlying flush of fever.

Emotionally, David had also changed. He no longer talked about God or religion or life in the hereafter, even to himself. It took too much energy to go through the details of anything so complex. Instead, he focused on the need to resist—he would never surrender, he would never put on the uniform. It was all he needed to know and all he was capable of dealing with. There were good reasons behind it, he was utterly convinced of that, but he was too tired, too sick, too alone to try to say what they were anymore, or to pay any attention to arguments against them. David was driven by unreasoning faith now, and arguments didn't matter.

His letter to Annie recited the bare facts of his situation. Essentially, a lawyer dictated the words to him, but the letter was made memorable by the way David closed it. "I love you, Annie," he said. Below that he carefully inscribed his name—David.

It was the first time he had ever uttered those words to her, or to anyone. Such an expression was foreign to their culture; it implied something too worldly. Hutterites have duties in this life, but they live for the hereafter.

David was ready to die for the Hutterite creed, but his mind was no longer occupied by the details and reasoning of it. It left an empty place, and thoughts of Annie and Joel had come to fill that place for him. These thoughts overwhelmed him as he penned the words to Annie, and a flood of happiness swept over him—happiness that his tormentors would have envied.

His stay at Fort Leavenworth was short and brutal. When he came off the train, his hands were still chained behind him, but there was enough slack in the chain so that he could carry his Bible. It and the clothes he wore were his only possessions. His new guards, a Mutt and Jeff pair, signed for him, took charge of his records, accepted the key to his chains, and pointed toward some distant buildings. "Your new home, scum," Mutt sneered. "Double time!"

"Double time," in army parlance, means to run rather than walk. David did his best to comply, but his chains made it difficult, and his weakness made him stagger. His arrival had been heralded, and soldiers along the way shouted abuse at him as his ragged, black-clothed figure reeled along the dusty road. After a few blocks, he staggered to a walk, but his guards were ready with persuaders. They jabbed his buttocks with bayonets until they got him into a crazy, drunken-looking trot again, and then tripped him.

Because of his chains, David went down hard, and the onlookers cheered. "Well, get up, you traitor fink," snarled Jeff, delivering a kick to David's ribs. "We got things for you to do here." They jerked him back to his feet when it became apparent that he couldn't get up alone, and started off again.

David was bloody, dirty, soaked with sweat, and essentially unconscious on his feet when they reached the prison gate. Inside the gate, his guards decided to clean him up a little before presenting him to the intake officer. A horse-watering tank struck them as being just the thing, so they grabbed him by the heels and shoulders and threw him in. The running water, supplied from a nearby well, was ice cold. David gave a gasp and a shudder as the last vestige of consciousness was driven from his body. The weight of his chains dragged him to the bottom, and he lay there in apparent repose while the two grinning apes watched with clinical interest.

"Guess we better pull the bastard out," one of them eventually decided. They deposited him on the muddy ground beside the tank, and waited for him to come around, prodding him occasionally with the tip of a bayonet to hurry the process.

"Hey, I don't think this shithead is even breathing," one of them finally exclaimed. "Mullins, you're a medic. Come over here and look at this piece of shit. I think maybe he got a little too much water."

Mullins, one of the gate guards, rushed over. "Get those damn chains off him, you assholes," he snapped, prying David's mouth open and rolling him over into position for artificial respiration. "Order a stretcher and blankets," he yelled to the other gate guard.

Mullins worked over David's prostrate form for several minutes before he was rewarded with a gasp and weak, labored breathing. There was no sign of consciousness, however, and Mullins shook his head as David was carried off to the prison dispensary. His Bible lay crumpled in the mud behind him. Mutt picked it up.

"I think I'll hang on to this. It might get me some laughs down at Molly's."

"Where d'ya get that 'me' shit? I've got as much right to it as you have."

"Okay, I'll flip you for the damn thing then. Call it." Mutt spun a coin into the air.

"Virulent pneumonia, plus a badly damaged heart, I would say." The prison doctor was speaking to the prison chaplain. "Undernourished besides, and there's probably brain damage from shock and lack of oxygen."

"I'm supposed to notify next of kin in all critical cases," said the chaplain. "Would you classify him as critical?"

"Hell, yes. I'll be surprised if he lasts until morning."

So it was that a telegram addressed to Annie came to the Gadsden depot the next morning. It was a form letter that the chaplain had worked up for such notices:

TO   MRS D HOFER GADSDEN HUTTERITE COLONY
      GADSDEN S DAK
FROM MAJ DERWAYNE SMITH CHAPLAIN U S ARMY
      U S ARMY MILITARY PRISON FT LEAVENWORTH
      KANSAS
REF   PRISONER PVT DAVID HOFER

SUBJECT INDIVIDUAL CONFINED TO PRISON INFIRMARY
IN CRITICAL CONDITION STOP YOU ARE ENTITLED TO
VISIT HIM WHILE THIS CONDITION LASTS STOP CONTACT
ME AT PRISON INFIRMARY UPON ARRIVAL IF YOU COME

The mailman delivered the telegram later that day. Preacher brought it to Annie, and they opened it together. She had already received the two letters. Paul's description of David's physical condition had prepared her. She prayed with Preacher as he suggested, but, by a terrible effort, she kept her emotions to herself in front of him.

The telegram was read at the evening religious service. Preacher announced that he and Annie would leave for Fort Leavenworth by train the next morning. He also indicated that more complaints had been presented to the secretary of war about treatment given to conscientious objectors at Leavenworth and elsewhere. The mood of the colony at the evening meal was grim. Was this to be déjà vu—Moravia repeated four centuries later? "We too must be strong."

Joel came to see Annie after supper. "My life is over," she said. "I feel sure they have killed David. I only want to be worthy of him—strong like him."

"Oh, Annie, please don't say that. I want to hope that David will come back to us. If they sent the telegram and have him in a hospital, it must mean they are trying to help him—someone there must be trying to help."

"Many people try, but the world is too evil."

There were tears in Joel's eyes again. "But Annie, why would anyone want to hurt us?"

"I don't know, Joel, but I know this. Our faith protects us from hurt because our life is in the hereafter, not here. They can't hurt a Christian."

"But Annie, you just said your life was over. You have a life here also, or at least you have had—with David, and with me, and with your family and everybody. Isn't that important too?"

Annie had no answer, but she was tearful, and gave Joel a little hug. "Yes," she finally said uncertainly. "I don't know. In some ways it would be easier to be true to our faith if we avoided life, but maybe it's already past the time when I can do that."

"I don't want you to leave me alone too," said Joel.

Preacher and Annie left the next day on the morning train. The afternoon mail brought another telegram—David was dead, as Annie's intuition had told her he was.

Joel was alone with his grief. He walked to a distant hayfield, hid behind a stack of alfalfa, and cried for hours. He was ashamed of his grief—there was no dignity in it, it was too worldly—but he was overwhelmed by it. Eventually, as the day wore on, an icy resolve began to form in his heart. He would never let anything like this happen to him again. Preacher was right. He would never cry again.

The telegram indicated that David's body could be returned to Gadsden if the next of kin were willing to pay shipping costs; otherwise it would be buried in a potter's field outside Fort Leavenworth. Decker immediately rushed to Gadsden and wired the money.

Preacher and Annie arrived at the prison gate three days after David staggered through it in chains. Within hours, the grim-faced pair was aboard another train headed for Kansas City, Omaha, and home. David's casket had already been shipped by freight and was somewhere ahead of them.

Decker had arranged to have a rig in Gadsden to meet every train. The casket arrived first, a plain wooden box, nailed shut. Six loaded it mournfully and returned to the colony. Decker ordered school closed, and the casket was placed on the floor in the middle of the room. It was left unopened, and three of the brethren were appointed to keep a silent vigil over it while awaiting the arrival of Preacher and Annie.

Finally, all of the adults of the colony were gathered into the room. "We believe that David is in heaven," intoned Preacher, "and that his remains are here before us. David died in defense of our principles. He was abused and tortured for two months for refusing to wear a military uniform, but he remained steadfast. He died in rags, but they were Hutterite rags.

"Elaborate ceremonies upon death are not our practice, because the remains are only clay, but we must look at David's body before it is interred. His family wishes this to be done in the presence of our prayers, and I agree that is proper."

He then led the group in a prayer while Jakela and Six came with tools, removed the nails, and tested the coffin lid to make sure it was loose. Annie, David's parents, and Preacher then came forward to set the lid aside.

Annie's eyes went to David's face first—and were riveted there. His face was sunken, thin, gray, and bruised. His eyes, black rimmed and drawn back into his head, stared obscenely in different directions. His beard was gone, as was most of his hair. The hair that remained had a sickly, dull matte appearance. Annie was instantly reminded of the decaying hide of a black horse that had died in the pasture last winter during a storm. Snow had buried it, and it had remained there until found in the spring. She gasped in shock.

The others gasped too, but for a different reason. An infuriated Preacher waved the rest of the group forward to look. Anger and outrage seethed through the homely room. In the argument between the military authorities and David Hofer, the guards at Fort Leavenworth had found a way to get in the last word. David's body was dressed in a soldier's uniform — the uniform of the United States Army.

The funeral was the largest Hutterite service ever held in America. Rumors about the bayonets, the beatings, and other mistreatment of conscientious objectors had been circulating for months, and examination of David's body confirmed the worst accounts. The Brethren swarmed to Gadsden from every colony in the Midwest. David was buried in a small fenced plot that Annie and Joel selected near the cottonwoods by the creek where they had each gone on so many early mornings to fetch the cows. They also selected a large fieldstone to mark the grave, and each of the sixteen colonies brought a smaller stone. These were evenly spaced in a circle around the large stone. Perhaps some future anthropologist will stumble upon David's grave and publish an article about an early Dakota culture that divided its day into sixteen hours of ninety minutes each.

A few weeks later, the Hutterites left David there alone. "We honor our dead, but our duty is to the living," said Preacher. "We cannot stay in a country that will torture our people for their beliefs. We must leave, whatever the cost.

"We should leave without malice toward our neighbors here. A society under stress demands conformity. This has always been true. Such demands, and the stress that prompts them, come from the evil world. Our neighbors are trapped in evil. We, as people of God, cannot yield to such evil, so conflict is inevitable. David Hofer was steadfast under the greatest adversity. We can only thank God for such a man and move on."

The Brethren agreed. Envoys were already in Canada, buying land, on the day of the funeral. The Hutterites would be allowed to live there in peace, said the Canadian government. An exodus started immediately and was complete by spring.

There were sixteen Hutterite colonies in America — fourteen in South Dakota and two in Montana. Only one chose to stay. The others boarded up the precious buildings they had so diligently constructed; left their carefully tilled acres to nature; loaded their property on wagons, trucks, and trains; closed their gates; and left for Canada to start a new life.

Annie and Joel visited David's grave together the day before they left. Indian summer had extended into November—the day was idyllic. Brown prairie grass crunched under their feet, and the air was heavy with goldenrod pollen. The cottonwoods along the creek still held their leaves, vast assemblages of honey-colored amber shrouds, fluorescent from the oblique sun.

Epilogue

After the exodus, visitors to David Hofer's grave were rare. Silence reclaimed its ancient own on the Gadsden prairie. The tiny plot would sometimes lie for years on end without having a human eye cast upon it. The once prosperous Gadsden colony site became a miniature ghost town on a bleak Dakota scene of dust bowl and depression in the 1930s.

THE ESSAY CONTEST

Country School

The page lay open and the boy stared at it in gentle awe. Jackie was eleven years old, he was barefoot, and he wore overalls. The book was new. Jennie Adkins, the county superintendent of schools, had left it there when she visited his school that morning. It was the *Course of Study* for all rural South Dakota schools for the school year 1935–1936. They would use the new book when school started again next fall. Jackie would be in the seventh grade then, if he passed.

"If he passed." He always added that qualification because his dad did, but it was a little joke between them. He would pass. There was still another day of school left after today (this was May 9), but he had already finished all of his two-day final examinations—they were easy. His teacher, Clarice, didn't write the test questions. The exams were standard and came from the state on nice printed forms. Since he was the only one in the sixth grade, she had let him go ahead with them at his own pace. He finished them all the first day, so he wouldn't have to come to school at all tomorrow, although the other kids would. There were ten other kids, and eight grades, in Jackie's one-room school, so being the only kid in a grade wasn't unusual.

Clarice wasn't much more than a kid herself—not twenty yet. This was her first year of teaching; after she finished high school she had attended Eastern Normal for one year to get her certificate. Clarice was a terror in "Kick the Can" games during recess—she was built low to the ground and charged like a Notre Dame fullback. Jackie had the lumps to show for these clashes on the playground.

Clarice was a local girl, but her parents lived several miles away, so she stayed at the Swansons'. They lived close to the school and didn't have children. Clarice always came early in the winter and had a fire going by the time the kids got there. She had some foolish rules, though, such as the one that the kids had to leave their lunch boxes in the unheated entryway-coatroom. On cold days the peanut butter sandwiches were frozen solid when noon came.

The new *Course of Study* drew Jackie's attention like a magnet. They seldom had anything new, and the old book was dog-eared from a year of use. That big book laid out everything they did, and he wanted to see if the new one changed anything. Like most kids, he listened in while the classes ahead of him were reciting, and he also liked to pore over the *Course of Study* to see what was coming up. It was kept on the teacher's desk, but he could use it, so he took the new one to his own desk and started paging through it.

He had looked ahead in the old book to what it showed for the seventh grade, so he had an idea of what to expect. Hilda and Otto were in the seventh now, and Jackie had been listening to them all year, so he had a head start anyway. The new book showed a lot of the same material, as he thought it would. There was long division in arithmetic and also some talk about written problems. History was in two units— South Dakota and United States. There was sentence diagramming in grammar, and the same spelling book they had been using, plus Palmer penmanship once a week. Science would be a new subject for him, but he knew what to expect from listening to Otto and Hilda, and to Ione in the eighth grade.

Jackie looked at what it said about science carefully, because it would be new. There was stuff about trees and plants that he remembered, and some about fish and other life in the ocean, and some about rocks. Suddenly, he saw there was something new—something that interested him a lot. The *Course of Study* was talking about the sun, the moon, the stars, and the planets. Only a few months earlier, Jackie had stumbled onto something about this in a book that his older sister brought home from high school. The concept fascinated him; he had never dreamed of such a thing. It had never occurred to him to wonder about where the sun really was or anything like that. The

Course of Study was very sketchy about it. For a moment, it made him anxious for fall to come.

The shiny newness of the book gave it a special smell. Jackie had closed it and was turning it over in his callused hands to admire its feel when he noticed the large print on the back cover. "Annual state-wide seventh-grade essay contest," it said. The subject for next year was "Rural Life in South Dakota." Last fall Clarice had tried to get Otto and Hilda to write something for the contest, but it didn't work out. The subject then had been "The Barberry Bush." The barberry bush was important as a host for a fungus that caused wheat rust, and the government had a big program to urge schoolchildren to find and destroy the bushes. But the farmers around Nunda raised corn and oats, not wheat. Nobody had ever seen a barberry bush there in the first place, so neither Otto nor Hilda knew what to write, and Clarice wasn't sure what a fungus was anyway.

Jackie took the book up to Clarice and showed her the part about the new contest. She encouraged him to think about it over the summer and to write an essay next year. It didn't have to be in until Christmas, so he had lots of time. She also said that she thought they had picked a much better subject this time. It was more general and could have different meanings in different parts of the state. Everyone would be able to find a topic they knew something about.

"Rural Life in South Dakota—hmm," she mused. Jackie could maybe write about jackrabbits. There were plenty of those around here. Clarice's view of the new topic was being colored by her experience with the barberry bush.

"Oh," said Jackie. You could tell he hadn't thought of jackrabbits. He went back and finished cleaning out his desk, and Clarice said that he might as well go on home if he wanted to. Since he had the pony, his younger brothers would be walking alone anyway. They would be along in an hour or so when school let out at four o'clock.

"Have a good time this summer," Clarice added. Jackie looked at Bobby and Roger. They were in the second and fourth grades, and it was nearly two miles to walk alone, but they were OK with it, so Jackie skipped out the door.

Otto

Teddy was standing patiently in the sun where Jackie had tethered him to the school yard fence that morning. He had eaten most of the grass he could reach. Teddy was big for a pony, and all black except for a small white pattern in the middle of his forehead. Jackie patted his neck and received a caress in return as Teddy rubbed the side of his head against Jackie's shoulder. He took the bridle bit willingly, then Jackie led him to the ditch alongside the driveway. By standing on the bank and clutching the mane with one hand, Jackie could swing himself up onto Teddy's bare back. Then they were off—loping down the edge of the road beside sunflowers that would be as high as a car in a few weeks.

They had learned to ride together, starting a year earlier when Teddy was two and had grown strong enough to carry a load. Jackie had never ridden a horse, and Teddy had never been ridden. There had been a lot of bruising falls, including one that had knocked Jackie unconscious for an hour or more, and purists scorned some of the techniques they had developed. Teddy was not "bridle-wise." Neither he nor Jackie understood the concept of "neck-reining." In spite of such gaps in their training they could do many things together now. They herded cows along the roadsides to save the meager grass in the pasture, and they rounded up the herd of work horses while the men were milking the cows in the early morning. They carried tools, lunches, and supplies across the fields and around the neighborhood. They even retrieved newborn calves from the far reaches of the farm, with the bawling calf draped across Teddy's back in front of Jackie, and the nervous mother cow trailing anxiously behind them.

Today, as they cantered along, Teddy's mind was on the barnyard and pasture at home. He wanted to roll in the dust and squirm on his back while he kicked his feet in the air, free. Along the way they passed a low spot where the ditch had been full of water earlier in the spring. A cloud passed over Jackie's face as he remembered an incident there, and its aftermath.

Jackie was walking home from school that day with Otto and some other kids. Otto was in a bullying mood. "Get down in the ditch, Jackie," he said. "You can walk down there. We don't want you Catholics walking up here on the road with us."

Jackie looked at the mud and water and ice in the ditch uncertainly, but Otto pointed imperiously. After a little hesitation, Jackie, as usual, did as Otto told him and came home shivering with the cold. His overalls and his long underwear were soaked to well above his knees, and his shoes were caked with mud and filled with muck and water.

Both of his parents were furious: Mother because of his clothes and because she was afraid he would get sick, Dad because Jackie would not stand up to Otto. "Why?" he demanded. "Why? Why do you let him push you around like that? There's no sense to it. Just tell him no. Tell him to walk down in the ditch himself if he wants someone to walk there. There's nothing he can do to you. He's only a year older than you, and not as strong as you are. You could beat him in a fight if you had to. But there would be no need of that anyway. He has never hit anybody, or hurt anybody physically, or even been in a fight that I've ever heard of. If he did try to hit you or push you, so what? He'd run home crying if you hit him back. This is your own fault. You ought to be ashamed of yourself."

Jackie was ashamed—and sad to think that he was such a disappointment to Dad. Everything that Dad said was right, but even so, similar things had happened since, and he hadn't stood up to Otto any more than he had that day by the ditch. He didn't know why, exactly. As far as getting hurt went, it was hard to imagine that Otto could hurt him as bad as he had been hurt by his falls from Teddy or by various other scrapes with livestock and equipment around the farm. As far as courage went, he was daring in the face of greater dangers—climbing the windmill, swinging from the haymow track, facing an angry cow guarding her newborn calf—many things.

But summer was coming, and he wouldn't have to deal with Otto anymore. Maybe things would be better next year. Otto would be in the eighth grade then—the highest grade. Most eighth graders seemed to have a sense of responsibility about their position, Jackie had noticed. They acted more dignified and grown up. Maybe Otto would too.

Dad was so upset after the ditch incident that he unburdened himself about it to a couple of neighboring farmers when the three of them were alone one day. Glen Weber was a man whom Dad respected for his opinions. He also liked to visit for the pure pleasure of listening to Glen's voice. Glen spoke in a slow nasal twang and peppered his conversation with colorful expressions.

Both men listened in silence and thought for a while after Dad had finished. Finally, Glen took his pipe from his mouth and let a billow of smoke drift skyward. "Waal, Jack, sounds to me as if you're raising yourself a Quaker there."

"Quaker! I doubt if he even knows what that is. I'm not too sure myself."

"Isn't that those guys that refuse to be in the army or salute the flag?" asked the other neighbor.

"There's others that do that too, but yeah, the Quakers are pacifists," answered Glen.

"Well, I don't like for the government to be telling people what to do," said the man, "but it seems to me if the country's in a war everybody ought to be bound to help. You were in France yourself, Glen. You know it's not just the soldier's war, it's everybody's war."

"Yeah, well, I know that one Christmas Eve the English soldiers and the German soldiers in the front lines left their trenches and met in no-man's-land to have a smoke together and a soccer game. I'm not so sure it's the soldier's war in the first place."

"You guys aren't really helping me a hell of a lot as far as my problem with Jackie. I want to know how you think somebody could have made him into a Quaker."

"I ain't saying anybody sold him on it, or even that he's ever heard the word. I just say it sounds as if he's come by their ideas naturally. And that ain't the worst. From what I understand, the Quakers have done a lot of good in this world."

"Well, Quaker or no Quaker, I don't see how anybody is ever going to make it in this world if they don't stand up for their rights," said Dad.

"Oh, they stand up for what's right, Jack. It's just that they generally come at it from some different direction."

Home

At supper on the night that Jackie finished school, they talked about the essay contest. There were ten people at the table, so it got a good going over. Art Carson was working there as the hired man, and the landlord, Emil Ordal, was there, as well as Alice, a neighbor girl, and Jackie's own family of seven. Alice was visiting Jackie's sister, Mary.

Emil, who was universally known as "Old Man Ordal," except to his face, was trimming trees on the farm. He had a bicycle with a sidecar and often would simply drop in and stay for weeks. He was quite deaf, so Art would often shout at him in Norwegian to get his attention.

Jackie and Art had a long-standing argument about cake. Jackie preferred white cake, so Art said that chocolate was better. It ended in a deal. When white cake was served, Jackie got two pieces and Art got none, and vice versa. Mother tolerated the agreement for a while, but she felt that she had to alternate white and chocolate cakes on successive bakings to keep it fair, and she was getting impatient with the whole thing. Tonight she had spice cake, which she said was neither white nor chocolate, so the deal was off. Mother added that this had gone on long enough anyway. Everyone should learn to like all kinds of food, she thought.

Mother had been a schoolteacher too. When Jackie came to the part about how Clarice had mentioned jackrabbits, she laughed and glanced knowingly at Dad. Maybe "Rural Life" could mean something different from Clarice's idea of it, she suggested. His essay could be about how people lived in rural South Dakota. In other words, Jackie could write about the people he knew, and what they did from day to day.

"But Clarice might not like that," said Mary. "You know how she is once she gets an idea." Mary and Alice went to high school at Rutland.

"It won't matter," said Mother. "She won't be there anyway. I think Ann Olson is going to teach that school next year."

Old Man Ordal had just finished his meal and was getting ready to drink his coffee. As usual, everybody stared in awe as he spooned two heaping teaspoonsful of sugar into the cup. But tonight Art had a little plan. He distracted Emil's attention to something outside the window, quickly piled in two more big spoonsful, and gave the coffee a good stir.

"My!" said Emil, wiping his mouth and beard with the palm of his hand after he drank. "That was sweet."

The Man from Boston

Jackie's Aunt Phyllis and Uncle Walt lived in Sioux Falls, and Aunt Phyllis came to visit quite often to see Grandma and everybody. When she came, she would sometimes bring them old magazines—*Collier's*, the *American*, the *Saturday Evening Post*, or *Ladies' Home Journal*. They had good stories to read, so Jackie often looked at them. He was surprised one day to find an article in the *American* called "Rural Life in Nebraska" by Alstair Wilson of Boston, Massachusetts.

The article talked about a woman named Willa Cather and said that life in Nebraska was very bad now. There were dust storms and abandoned farms, and the people lived like animals, it said. A terrible, terrible life. It described outdoor privies and houses without electricity or running water, as if they were something unusual. There was a picture of an abandoned farm with the dust blowing across. The Hattleberg farm, two miles to the west, looked like that picture, especially in late March after the snow was gone and the dust blew. It had been empty for many years. Jackie and Roger thought it was haunted.

The "black blizzards" that the article described were real enough. Last summer one came and piled the soil into drifts like small snowbanks along the fence lines and around the buildings. So much soil seeped into the attics of some houses that the ceilings broke down.

But the article sounded as if it was that way all the time, as if the author had never been to Nebraska—as if he had only read about it and had some wrong ideas.

My essay is not going to talk so much about this stuff, thought Jackie. It would be better if I told how it is most of the time. He went back to the part about the "terrible, terrible life" and read it again and wondered about it. He imagined that Nebraska would be a lot like South Dakota, but his life didn't seem terrible to him. Of course, he had never been to Boston. He had cousins in Sioux Falls, though, and had been there. He did have fun, but he wasn't at all sure that he would want to live there. And his relatives from Sioux Falls always enjoyed visiting Nunda and the farm.

There was another picture, showing three little boys, obviously brothers, huddled together. They were peering forlornly out of the page like gophers from a hole. The boys badly needed haircuts and looked just like a family Jackie had seen at the barbershop last winter. Those boys obviously hadn't been to town for months and were in awe of the strange surroundings. He and Roger and Bobby looked like that sometimes too, Jackie realized, and Otto used it against him. The picture could almost have been of them, but they weren't really very much like the image it projected.

The man from Boston also talked about the schools in Nebraska. He compared them to schools in places like Boston. The country schools represented another terrible situation, he said. How could a child possibly learn anything—cooped up in a forlorn shack on the windswept prairie with an immature teacher whose only education beyond a substandard high school was one year at a small normal school? This part of the article bothered Jackie, but he was afraid to tell anyone; it might sound like complaining. He looked around in the magazines for something better and did see a little article in the business section. It told about a growing company in St. Paul that it said was a rare bright spot in the economic picture. The company was called the Minnesota Mining and Manufacturing Company; it made tape and sandpaper and some other stuff. The good part for Jackie was that the man who ran the company was from White, South Dakota, not far from Nunda. His name was William McKnight, and his only education had been country school and high school in White. Maybe country school wasn't so bad.

Summertime

School, and Otto, were almost forgotten as May moved toward June. Jackie was learning to milk cows that summer and toiled long and hard while hunched against the cow's side on a one-legged stool. He was slow, and his forearms ached from the effort for several weeks, but his grip and his skill gradually improved. It was not his favorite job.

The cow barn could be a pleasant place in the winter, snug and secure, kept warm by the heat from the bodies of all the animals there. The milking and feeding were done after supper in the dim light of a kerosene lantern. On Sunday nights, chores were delayed until after seven o'clock, when the Jack Benny program on the battery-powered radio was over. Jackie and his brother Roger each had a favorite cow, and they would often lie on the back of their cow, half drowsing in the semidarkness, while the men finished their chores or sat and talked.

The cow barn in the late afternoon in the summer was another matter—stifling hot, smelly, and thick with flies. Grass-fed cows defecate a product that is more liquid than solid, and the flanks and the bushy tails of the cows were often soaked with it. The sweat-drenched milker huddled close against the cow's flank, which radiated heat like a furnace, and tried to dodge the juicy switching tail.

Decoration Day (officially known as Memorial Day) came on Thursday that year. As usual, the community turned out for it. After morning chores, the whole family got out of their farm clothes and into town clothes and piled into the 1929 Pontiac. The Badus Cemetery was scheduled first, so Dad headed west and parked in the country churchyard that served the parish and the one-room country school adjacent to it. Several cars were already there, and people were walking the short distance down the road to the graveyard. Jackie's mother and the other ladies of the Legion Auxiliary had already put wreaths on the graves of the former soldiers buried there.

Other people came and joined them; then two cars pulled up to the gate, and the firing squad members got out and organized them-selves with flags and rifles, ready to march out onto the field. Jackie, and everyone else, knew the men well. They were veterans of the Great War, which later came to be known as World War I, and were in their late thirties. It was strange to see them march—"prancing like stud horses," someone always said, and quite a show for Jackie and his brothers. After a public prayer, the squad fired their rifles out over the graves and the lake, and then got ready to move on to the next ceme-tery. Some of the men brought a self-important air to their role, while others were embarrassed by this moment in the public eye.

Afterward, Dad was visiting with John McCabe and Mother was looking around the cemetery. Joe McCabe, John's brother, was one of the men in the firing squad. Joe and John were both bachelors, and friendly guys. They had a big farm, inherited from their father, who had homesteaded it, and Jackie liked to ride Teddy up to their place and visit with them.

Bobby went with Mother on her tour of the cemetery, but Jackie and Roger ran back to the churchyard and its playground. Other kids were there, and one of them had a ball, so they played catch and swung on the swings until it was time to go. It was fun to be away from Otto's tyranny and play at a different school with different kids.

They drove into Nunda for a program held in the hall upstairs over the café in a building that used to be a hotel. When the firing squad came back after visiting the last cemetery, everybody assembled in the hall. The program, as always, included a recitation of "In Flanders Field." Mrs. Evans read a short essay on "Peace" that she had written for "All Go Club" last year. There were recitations and songs by other kids, including "If You Want Any More You Can Sing It Yourself," by little Lyman Tenning, and a speech by a man who was a relative of the Ordal family. He was a minister or something and lived in Minneapolis.

The program brought Jackie's mind, and that of his mother, back to the essay contest. They were going to Madison anyway, and Madison had a public library. Mother suggested he look in the encyclopedia for some background information. Maybe something about how many people lived on farms, or where they came from.

"Grandma's dad and mother came from Ireland when they were little kids," chimed in Roger. "She told me one day when I was looking at a picture on her wall."

"That's right," said Mother. "Then they lived in Iowa, and your grandmother and grandfather were one of the first families to homestead here."

As they always did when they got to Madison, Jackie, Roger, and Bobby went to the courthouse to use the toilets. It was a considerable luxury for them—a sit-down toilet that flushed and a washbowl with hot and cold running water, liquid soap, and paper towels. There was nothing like this on the farm, or in Nunda. Jackie remembered that the man from Boston had talked about outdoor toilets in his article. It was hard to imagine having something like this right in the house, but he had to admit that it would be nice in the winter.

The toilet at home was the standard outhouse, set over a pit dug in the ground. Periodically, it was moved to a new pit a few feet away, and the old pit was filled with soil and covered over. Last year's Montgomery Ward catalog for toilet paper was traditional and provided interesting reading material as well. Actually, except on cold winter nights, the outhouse wasn't bad. It had a small hole in the door, like a nail hole, and you could glue your eye to it and observe the world on the other side as you sat there in the semidarkness. It seemed as if you were looking out at a scene from a place that was detached and remote from the everyday world on the other side of the peep hole. It gave Jackie a strange feeling of exhilaration to observe the world through that hole. Years later, he found a similar experience described in a story he read.

The Fourth of July was exciting too, with a trip to town a couple of days in advance for firecrackers. There were also sparklers, Roman candles, and skyrockets, which the boys carefully saved until the night of the third. The firecrackers went into action at once, frightening Laddie, the collie, and sending chickens and geese squawking for cover. Tin cans and firecrackers furnished Jackie and Roger with endless diversion for a couple of days.

The whole family went to Lake Campbell for the afternoon and evening of the Fourth, as they did every year. The hood ornament that held five little American flags was fastened to the radiator cap of the Pontiac, and off they went down the road with the three little hills that Dad always took at just the right speed to bring everyone's stomach into his throat.

Grandma and others from the family were already there and had staked out a picnic table for group headquarters. Lake Campbell had swimming, firecrackers, swings, boat rides, softball, roller-skating in the pavilion, a big picnic, and a fireworks display after dark. No one could possibly ask for more.

I'm going to write about today in my essay, thought Jackie before he fell asleep in the backseat as the Pontiac made its way home.

A few weeks later, harvest had begun and everyone was very busy. One evening after supper, Dad told Jackie to ride the pony over to Hubmans' farm to pick up some sickle sections for the grain binder. Ernest Hubman, who was Otto's father, had offered to pick them up when he was at the machinery store, to save Dad the trip.

Jackie arrived as the Hubmans were finishing supper and getting ready to start the milking and other evening chores. Mrs. Hubman (Beret) invited Jackie to sit down and have some waffles and ham, but he thanked her and said he had just finished supper. Outside, the Hubman men and Otto stopped to admire Teddy. Otto didn't have a pony, and Jackie had never seen him ride.

The Hubman farm was large, as was the family. This was a second marriage for both parents. Otto's half brothers and half sisters were grown men and women, and several of them worked on the farm with their parents. They were busy people, and everything about the Hubman place was always clean, ship-shape, and freshly painted, if compared to other farms around the neighborhood.

Jackie put the box of sickle sections on a stump near the fence post where he had tethered his pony, and walked to the barn with the

Hubmans to watch them milk. He always liked to see their modern barn with its steel stanchions and its concrete floors and gutters. Most barns, including his, had dirt floors, and the cows were tied to wooden mangers with neck chains.

He and Otto stood and watched as the men bustled about. The cows came into their assigned places, the barn was sprayed for flies, and the milking began. Jackie was surprised, as he always was when he came here, by the fact that Otto didn't seem to have anything to do. At home, there was never enough help, and Jackie was kept busy all of the time. Here, the men did everything. Otto acted as if he wanted to help, but didn't really know how, and the men seemed to brush him impatiently aside.

At school, Otto talked about "Papa" all of the time. "Papa said this," and "Papa said that," he would tell the teacher several times a day. Papa went here, and Papa went there. Here, at home, Papa didn't seem to say much of anything, at least not to Otto.

Otto was different here too. There was hardly any of his usual bluster and no sign of his bullying tactics. It seemed as if he was uncertain, almost as if he wanted to be friendly. It wouldn't last, though, Jackie was pretty sure of that. He had been at the Hubmans' and seen this side of Otto before.

Nunda

A lone grasshopper jumped from the sidewalk into the dusty street as Jackie made his way toward the pool hall. He had a nickel in his pocket, but he didn't hurry—the ice cream bars would be there when he was ready. He could savor the thought of it for a while first.

What Jackie knew about nickels had come hard. That was two years ago, on a Sunday. There had been a baseball game in town, and they had come in to watch. The Nunda team was playing Castlewood. He liked to see so many people together, and to watch and listen. The cars were always pulled up around the field, and people sat in them with the doors open, or on the fenders and running boards, or on the grass, or stood around. There were no bleachers, nor any beepers or buzzers on the cars. It was comfortable and easy.

After the game, the teams and their fans went up on Main Street to visit. Jackie and his brothers asked Dad for money, and he fished in his pocket and came up with a nickel for each, while continuing to talk with Ole Elverud and Joe McCabe. It was the first spending money that Jackie had seen for a long time. Roger and Bobby headed for the café, probably for Popsicles. Jackie started to follow, but his eye was also on the new place across the street in a small building that had always been empty before. Roosevelt had been elected, Prohibition was over, and Henry Hyland ("Rats") had opened the Nunda Bar.

The small room was full as Jackie made his way in through the screen door that day. Nobody paid much attention to him, but a couple of the men that he knew waved a friendly hello. He had made his way to the candy counter and studied the display carefully. Mr. Goodbar was new then. His older sister had given him part of one once, and he remembered it well. A huge candy bar with a bright yellow wrapper, it was made of little squares of chocolate and small peanuts. His mouth had watered as he gazed at the box on display. That was it, he had decided; nothing else could really compare. He took his nickel out of his pocket and held it up against the glass.

Rats was very busy, though, and couldn't get down to that end of the bar right away. The beer was flowing freely, and everyone wanted to know about his new business. Then a big farmer backed up a step or two to let someone else up to the bar and forced Jackie away from the counter. Jackie's nickel was still in his hand, and he was looking for a way to get back up to the candy counter when his attention was distracted by the slot machines. They were new to Nunda, but Jackie had heard of them before. Rats had a brown penny machine and a gleaming chrome nickel machine with a glass window full of more nickels than Jackie had ever seen before. As he looked at it a man came up and put in a nickel. When he pulled the lever the drums of pictures spun around and around, then clicked to a stop, one by one. Two oranges and a cherry! The machine clunked and spit two nickels into the tray. The man laughed and scooped them into his hand.

Jackie stood, with his nickel in his hand, staring at the window full of nickels. Robotlike, he put his nickel into the slot and pulled the lever. This time the drums clicked to a stop with two lemons and an orange showing. After another hollow clunk, it sat there silent. The counter had cleared a little, and the candy bars were there, suddenly as distant from Jackie as the moon. Tears rose to his eyes, but he pulled his head down into his shoulders and slid out the door. To this day, no one else knew.

But today he had his nickel, and he had some time. Mother had let him come into town with her when she came in to put up the mail. After Roosevelt had become president in 1933, Dad had been appointed as postmaster of Nunda because he was about the only Democrat around. It didn't amount to much money, but he was glad to have it. Times were hard in Dakota in 1935, very hard. During the crop-growing season, Mother did the postmaster work more often than Dad because he was usually working in the fields. It only took an hour or two.

Nunda was small, although it didn't seem that way to Jackie. It had streetlights when they ran the generator, which they always did on Saturday night. There were five streetlights, plus a Peerless Beer neon sign on the pool hall that could be seen all the way from their farm, more than two miles away.

Saturday night in Nunda in the summer was enchanting; the main street was lined with parked cars along its entire two-block length. Everybody was there. The barbershop was overflowing with men with a week's growth of beard; Ivan Berge and Elmer Loner bustled around in their competing grocery stores, buying eggs and cream and selling groceries; pool balls clicked under hooded lights on five tables in Jim Faiferlick's pool hall; and people gathered and talked everywhere. Sometimes they had free outdoor movies, projected against the north wall of the old hotel building.

Fats Hanneman was in the pool hall one Saturday night when Jackie went in to watch the games and listen to the talk. He didn't know Fats, had only heard the name. Other people knew him, though, because he used to live here. He lived in Detroit now, and worked in a car factory, but came back from time to time because he was courting Martha Kuehl.

Fats was kind of dressed up, compared to everybody else, and seemed to have a lot of money. He was a little bit drunk and was talking a lot. Several men were gathered around him. (Women didn't go into the pool hall.) Jackie moved closer to listen.

Fats was making fun of Nunda—of the dirt street, of the outhouses, of the dollar-a-day wages. He sneered about the snowbound farms and the blizzards in the winter, and about the black blizzards in the summer, and about the guys on WPA loading gravel trucks by hand with a shovel. He didn't mention the country schools—you could tell he probably didn't spend much time thinking about schools.

Some younger guys hung their heads and said, yeah, they'd been thinking about getting out of here too, and going to California. Joe McCabe looked the visitor in the eye and asked if there was any WPA in Detroit. Joe was a war veteran and knew quite a bit about city life. Actually, Joe said, he thought he had even seen pictures in the paper of breadlines in Detroit a few weeks ago. "Or was that Cleveland?" he asked Fats, with a wink at Jackie. "Yeah, it was probably Cleveland," mumbled Fats.

But this was not Saturday night, this was Thursday morning, getting toward noon. Nunda was mostly empty under the hot July sun as Jackie moved on toward the pool hall. "Telephone Central," Mrs. Emmons, was at the switchboard as Jackie passed her open door. He stopped to watch as she answered a ring. Central's ring was a long and a short. Mrs. Emmons said, "Nunda," listened briefly, and plugged some cords across the board. After that, she rang, said, "There you are," and listened briefly again. Then she pulled her plug, hung up the headset, and went into her kitchen. Jackie went on toward the pool hall.

He paused as he passed the old hardware store building and wondered about Joe Whitehorse. Joe bought pop bottles. He and Roger took six bottles they had found up to Joe's room one time, and had received a penny apiece for two of them. Mother was displeased; she muttered something about "bootleggers." The hardware store itself was empty, but Joe still had his room upstairs and in the back. He worked for McCabes most of the time, but lived in town.

The empty hardware store was typical. In 1915 Nunda had a doctor, a drug store, a hotel, and a bank, among other businesses. On the surface the town had changed very little, but the hotel was empty, the drug store had become Hannah's Café, the doctor had left town, and the bank had gone broke. Prohibition had, of course, intervened, but it was gone now, and, in any case, Nunda had not slavishly followed every detail of its complex restrictions.

Joe Whitehorse had understood the complexities of the law against alcohol about as well as anybody. During Prohibition, men could often be seen going up to his room to have it explained. Joe was a personable guy and had a different accent; his real name was Joseph

Woitkelewicz. Jackie's dad claimed to be the only man in town who knew how to spell Joe Whitehorse's name. John McCabe said that Joe was Polish. Jackie wasn't sure what that was, but he knew that most people were Lutheran.

Jackie didn't know it, but Nunda, only twenty-five years old, was already far past its prime. The trend that had taken away the doctor and the bank and the livery stable was continuing. After cars became common, these services had been eliminated or concentrated into the larger towns. Nunda was dying, as were thousands of towns like it. A good way of life was dying with them, and many were sorry to see it go.

A wooden bench sat on the sidewalk, facing the dusty street outside the pool hall. On warm summer days it was the gathering place for ancient local philosophers. The bench was full today. Hans Alfson, Poker Ole, Bill McGinty, Sarge, and Jim Faiferlick were there, and the argument was on. Listening was one of Jackie's greatest pleasures, and he needed ideas for his essay anyway. He had noticed that he could sometimes get new ideas by listening to people talk. And did these guys ever talk!

Jackie had that right. If he wanted to hear talk, this was the place to come. These guys could argue, often effectively, about anything. Every subject had two or more sides. They excoriated Roosevelt and Hoover before him. Hail insurance, the state cement plant, the Wobblies, and crop rotation all received detailed consideration along with John D. Rockefeller, Henry Ford, and the banking system.

The rules were unwritten but carefully followed. Nobody interrupted. Presentations were short and to the point. The speakers thought before they spoke.

After each sally there was a short period of reflective silence followed by scathing counterpoint from farther down the bench. They pulled no punches as they addressed the subject. Nothing was said about the motives or personality of the previous speaker. On any topic that could be stated, someone would rise to the bait, and the fight was on.

One subject, however, won universal agreement; no one was foolhardy enough to take issue with it. It came to constitute a sort of closing ritual. As the day wore on to a certain point the discussion would slow, and someone would glance at the position of the sun in the sky. A short period of silence would follow, and then he would say:

"Yep, the thing that ruined the country was the automobile."

Nothing further was ever said; they contemplated this universal truth for a moment or two, spat reflectively into the dust, rose, and went their separate ways.

Jackie watched them go; then he entered the pool hall. It was cool and dark after the hot sun outside. His callused bare feet snuggled into the sawdust on the floor. The long room was dark after the glare of the sun, and the empty tables receded into the distance like a row of dominoes. The racks of cues and balls along the wall, and the row of chairs beneath them, reminded him of a row of telephone poles that marched off over a hill west of the farm. The pool hall was empty except for Bogie, who stood behind the bar. Jackie put his nickel on top of the glass candy counter.

"I'll take an ice cream bar," he said.

"Maybe I can dig around here and pick out one with a pink center," said Bogie. "Think you could eat two?"

Jackie smiled, but he didn't really get his hopes up. He knew that some bars did have pink ice cream, and that meant a second one free, but he had never had one. Roger did get a free Popsicle once, though. One of the sticks of the orange Popsicle he bought had the words "Free Popsicle" printed on it. He had given Jackie half of the second one.

The School Board

One Wednesday night in August there was a school board meeting at Jackie's house. One-room country schools like Jackie's were scattered across the countryside every few miles and grouped into school districts. Technical supervision for the teachers came from the county superintendent, but a three-man school board hired, fired, and paid the teachers and otherwise administered each district. Dad was on the school board.

Mother made coffee and lemonade, and was baking some cookies that the boys eyed hungrily, but the cookies were for the school board and off limits. Before the meeting actually started, the three men talked farming, and did a lot of joking about the teachers' "systems." Jackie wasn't sure what they were talking about.

What it was, was this: the educators in the state were involved in a big argument about the best way to teach the kids. Two systems were in vogue. The Mork System favored close state control of the curriculum, while the Alfred System called for more local input.

It seemed to these three farmers that the teachers and the county superintendent were obsessed with this esoteric subject. Every time they had to talk to any of them about anything, they ended up listening to a lecture about the advantages of one damn system or the other.

They listened carefully and pretended to regard the question as one of some importance, but this was a facade. For some of them, formal schooling had ended with the fourth grade, and this whole argument struck them as pretentious, time-wasting nonsense. "If two and two make four, why the hell can't they just say so?"

Working for Joe

For the first time in his life, Jackie got a job that summer. In one sense, he had always had a job—but that was at home. This time, Joe Nelson came up one day and asked Dad if he could hire Jackie for a few days. They were stacking hay in the field and needed someone to rake after the bucker. Joe had a gentle old team of black horses for the rake, and both he and Dad thought Jackie could do it well enough, so it was agreed. Nothing was said about wages, although Jackie knew that the Nelsons were, if anything, even shorter of money than his own family was. Joe and Lloyd were brothers in their early twenties; their father had died two years earlier. The Nelsons were close friends of the family anyway, and Joe was very outgoing.

Joe and Lloyd had hired another man too, so there was a crew of four—three men plus Jackie. He started on Wednesday afternoon. After that, he walked to the Nelson farm each morning after breakfast and worked there all day. Mrs. Nelson was quiet and friendly and always had a good dinner and supper for them.

The work was hard, although Jackie's part of it wasn't bad. The hay had previously been raked into windrows that stretched across the field. The hay bucker is like a giant tine scoop that slides along the ground between the two horses that pull it. The driver guides the horses down the windrow until the bucker fills itself, and then heads them to the spot where the stack is being made. The load is left there by backing the bucker away from it, and a man pitches it up onto the stack with a pitchfork. The third man, who also has a pitchfork, is on top of the stack, building it in such a way that it will stand and shed rain. The bucker always spilled some hay, or failed to pick some of it up, so Jackie was supposed to rake the hay that the bucker missed into a new windrow. He and the bucker operator would also help pitch hay up onto the stack when they had time.

All four of them shared other, incidental, tasks. The horses had to be harnessed and hitched, fed and watered. The simple machinery had to be oiled, greased, and fixed when it broke.

On Friday, they castrated twenty-five recently weaned pigs before they went back to the field after the noon meal. Before they started, Lloyd poured two gallons of creosote dip into a fifty-five-gallon barrel full of water. A flat board nailed to a partition in the pen served as the operating table. Joe did the actual surgery with a sharp jackknife. Jackie and Lloyd took turns. Each would catch a pig, carry it to the operating table, and hold it while the surgeon did his duty. Some of the pigs were almost too much for Jackie, so he tried to catch smaller ones and leave the biggest ones to Lloyd. The technique was to wrestle the pig onto its back and hold one hind leg in each hand.

It was a squealing, squalling, messy affair, and hard work. When surgery was complete, Jackie's next duty was to pick the pig up by its hind legs and plunge it bodily into the fifty-five-gallon barrel. The creosote dip solution served a double purpose: it disinfected the site of the surgery, and it also took care of any skin parasites that the pig had acquired.

From Jackie's perspective, the good thing about the plunge into the barrel was that it put an abrupt end to the ear-splitting squeals. The bad thing was that the splashing drenched him with the dip solution. It smelled and tasted terrible, and stung his eyes and skin. He knew from helping Dad with this job that it was best to hang tight on to the pig when it went into the barrel so that you could pull it out again. Otherwise, they were hard to get ahold of in there, and it always seemed as if they might bite.

Saturday night was payday, and there was a festive mood because everybody was going to town. "Well, I gotta pay the hired man," said Joe. "What do you figger you got comin', Jackie?"

"Oh, I dunno," Jackie replied, suddenly embarrassed.

"Well, you're eleven. I know some kids your age have been getting a quarter a day," said Joe. "But you should have a little more because you've done such a good job."

"Oh, a quarter would be plenty," said Jackie.

"Well, let's call it a dollar even," suggested Joe.

"That would be too much," said Jackie. "We only worked a little on Wednesday."

They finally dickered it out at ninety cents and were both uncomfortable with the result. Jackie showed the money to Mother when he got home.

"Oh, you shouldn't have taken so much," she said. "Think of how they fed you and everything."

"I know, but they were going to give me even more," he said, feeling ashamed.

"Well, it's all right then. But you shouldn't expect to always get so much. They're neighbors, and we should be willing to help them when we can. Earl Wolff is doing farm work for thirty dollars a month, and he's a very good worker and a married man. Of course, they get board and room too, such as it is."

School Again

As August drew toward its end, threshing was over and there was no need to herd the cows anymore. They had become gleaners and grew fat grazing the fields of oat stubble, where pigeon grass shot up after a recent rain and was supplemented by grass and grain along the fence lines and by oats that the harvest had missed.

School was getting ready to start, and Mother took Jackie, Roger, and Bobby on a shopping trip to Madison in preparation. Shoes were to be worn from the outset this year, and the first order of business was to force three hardened, brown pairs of feet into alien confinement. As a concession to being the littlest one, and a boy who took care of his things, Bobby got a painted lunch bucket. Jackie and Roger would continue to use half-gallon syrup pails, except that Jackie often took a sack instead when he rode Teddy.

Mother helped select pencils and tablets. Roger and Bobby each got a new set of color crayons, and Jackie came up with an important-looking compass and protractor. There were new overalls too, and two new shirts for each boy. Another chapter of life was about to begin, and they were ready. In the excitement, Jackie had almost forgotten about Otto and the essay. He had plenty of time for the essay, though; it wasn't due until Christmas.

On the appointed day three freshly scrubbed boys, new from the skin out, set off down the country road together. Mother watched them go and thought of a long-ago day when she and her sister had gone down that same road on that same mission. A tear clouded her eye for a moment before she turned to her pile of laundry.

The new teacher was a big change from Clarice. Ann was quiet and kind and didn't play "Kick the Can." She got thirty dollars a month too, but not room and board like Earl Wolff and his wife. Ann stayed at the Swansons', as Clarice had. They didn't charge her anything, although she was expected to help Karen with her work.

Otto, however, was worse than ever. Ann's style seemed to encourage him, and his idea of the eighth grade was that it made him boss over all of the younger kids. He took Bobby's new lunch bucket, scooped it full of cow shit, and heaved it into the swamp while Jackie stood helplessly by. They washed it out in the stock tank where the horses and cows drank, straightened the bent handle, and hoped that Mother wouldn't notice. Bobby didn't tell, and Jackie was glad of that because he knew that Dad would have raged at him for not protecting Bobby. He felt bad about asking Bobby to keep secrets from Mother, though.

All through that fall and winter, recess was hell for Jackie. They played outside, and Otto made up rules to exclude him from practically every game. If they played softball, he was sent to the other end of the school yard to stand forlornly hitting a mark on a post with a stick. It was supposed to improve his aim because he didn't bat well enough.

Snow came early that winter, and strong winds created big drifts they could tunnel into to make caves and forts. One day when Jackie was lying on his back at the end of a narrow tunnel, extending it, Otto caved the tunnel in from above. Buried in snow with his arms pinned to his sides, Jackie was unable to move or even cry out. Panic overtook him. Luckily, there was less snow around his feet and legs, and he was able to raise his knees. This allowed him to kick and thrash enough to roll and get one shoulder up to free his arm so that he could claw his way out. He was still sobbing, choking, and screaming when he got to his feet. The smirk on Otto's face showed satisfaction. It was the first time he had ever really "gotten to" his quarry. After that day, Jackie lost what remained of the sympathy he had briefly felt for Otto the summer before.

The Solar System

One afternoon in early September the school board came around on its annual visit to the schools in the district. They first walked carefully around the school building, studying the roof and windows. Then they briefly turned their attention to the outhouses, the coal shed, and the fence around the yard. Satisfied with what they found, they came into the school to look around, and gave special attention to the heating stove, removing the grate to inspect it and probing the stovepipe with the point of a jackknife. That done, they greeted the kids and talked with Ann to find out how things were going and whether she had any problems.

Things were going pretty well, Ann said, although she did have one problem. The *Course of Study* for the seventh grade this year included a study of the sun and of the earth, moon, and stars. It called for the use of a certain book, and this book came with some foldout charts that showed the orbits of the planets and their moons. She didn't have this stuff, and she needed it to teach her seventh grader (Jackie) about the solar system. Could she order it?

Well, they really had no money at all. The order for books had been trimmed to the very minimum when they went over it with Jenny early in the summer. They understood how important it was, but what she was talking about was quite expensive, more than four dollars, and they didn't know where it could come from. They were going to have a meeting next week, though, and they would look at this to see if there was any possible way.

Dad tried to stay out of this discussion as much as possible, because it involved his kid. He could see that Stanley Hoffman was growing very impatient with it anyway, so they left. When they got outside, they immediately found out what the problem was. "Goddamn it, Jack," groused Stanley. "Just when I thought we had this fool thing straight. Now what in the hell system is this 'solar' system?"

The Essay

The essay contest was still on Jackie's mind, so he talked to Ann about it one day after school started. She said that she was glad to hear that he already knew about it. Jenny Adkins had brought it up at a teachers' meeting in Madison, and she had some more material about it. No kid from Lake County had ever won it, or even come close, so Jenny was anxious to get entries. There was going to be a county contest this year, in addition to the state contest. The three best essays from the county would be read at the county fair next August and would get prizes of ten, five, and two dollars. The essay had to be five hundred words or more, but they thought that a thousand words would be better.

A thousand words! "How long would that be," Jackie wondered. Ann didn't know, but she suggested that he count the words in a chapter in his history book—that should give him a pretty good idea. He tried, but he lost track and had to start over. Finally, he got out his tablet and started counting a page at a time and writing the number down. It turned out there were 847 words in Chapter 2, and 1,129 in Chapter 3, if he counted numbers and everything. He wondered how many tablet pages he would have to write, so he copied part of one chapter into his tablet and found that he got about 55 words on a page. "You probably get more on a page when you copy it that way than you will when you have to make it up," suggested Ann.

"Looks as if I'm going to need about twenty good pages," Jackie figured.

They talked about it at home that night. Jackie's sister said that she was taking typing at high school and could maybe learn enough by then to be able to type it, if he ever really got it done. Mary sounded skeptical, but typing sounded really important to Jackie, so he got out a pencil and paper after supper and started making a new list of things that could be in the essay. Mary was interested in the contest and said he would have to give her part of the prize for typing it if he won. Jackie said OK. He really wasn't thinking much about the prize, because he didn't really imagine there was any chance he would win. He was more interested in the essay itself. He wanted to write something that would give a true picture. He still thought that the article about Nebraska by the man from Boston wasn't fair.

"Why don't you talk to Grandma and get her to tell you what it was like when she came here?" suggested Mother.

Jackie worked hard on the essay all through September and October. Both Ann and Mother watched the result with interest. At first, they both thought he was doing it wrong. He didn't have much in it about history or about what crops were raised or how many schools there were or any statistics. Instead, he just described what he and other people did from day to day, and tried to explain how they felt. The more he worked on the essay, the more they got interested in it.

"Well, it won't win any prizes, but that's rural life in South Dakota all right," Mother said. "It seems funny to see it written down."

Shortly before Thanksgiving, Jackie counted his words again, got 1,063, and decided the essay was finished. He got some theme paper, recopied it as neatly as possible, and then turned it over to Mary for typing. Ann was planning the annual school Christmas program and decided to have Jackie read part of the essay there. This was something new.

The format of the Christmas program had always been rigid. The front of the schoolroom was curtained off to make a stage, the desks were moved aside, and planks borrowed from the lumberyard were set up on blocks to serve as seats for the audience. In this makeshift theater, the kids put on a little play, sang some songs, and performed as a stick band while the teacher accompanied them on the organ. The instruments for the stick band were standard issue to all country schools and consisted mostly of pairs of roughened sticks that could be rapped or rubbed together. There was also a steel triangle that was held, suspended by a string, in one hand, and struck with a small metal rod. The other piece consisted of three bells on a strap that was wrapped around the hand and shaken like a castanet. The triangle and the bells went to students deemed to possess musical talent.

Jackie was not one of these. He was in the seventh grade, but he was still, and would always be, in the stick section—assigned to the blue sticks this year. He didn't think he could sing very well either, and Clarice had always agreed. Last year, when they were rehearsing "Jingle Bells" and "Silent Night" for the Christmas program, she had acted decisively.

"Just stand there and move your lips, Jackie," she said. "People will think you are singing."

Now, for a substantial part of the big evening, all eyes would be on Jackie. He was determined to make a good showing. "Which part of my essay will I read?" he asked Ann.

"Well, I'm not sure," she said. "Why don't you make a list of some of the different things you wrote about, and then try to pick out parts that sound interesting by themselves and that you could read in about five minutes. You could read the list of subjects first, and then tell them which parts you have selected for the program."

"OK," he said. This is Jackie's list:

Country School	Teddy
Home	The Man from Boston
Summertime	Nunda
The School Board	Working for Joe

Everyone at the Christmas program enjoyed the essay. They had coffee and cake and Christmas cookies afterward, and the adults all stopped him to say it was good and to laugh about different things in it.

Ernest Hubman, Otto's father, was especially complimentary. He was a large, heavy man, dressed in new overalls. The plank seat was too low for him, so he sat somewhat awkwardly with his knees spread apart and his overshoe-clad feet splayed out. Dad was seated beside him; they were drinking coffee and talking about the price of oats. Otto was standing beside his father, attempting to demonstrate the triangle he had played, but Ernest was ignoring him—almost brushing him aside with the back of his hand as he bent to listen to what Dad was saying.

Ernest's face lit up when Jackie happened by. "Yackie!" he said. "That was sehr gut! We'll hear it again at the fair next summer, don't you think?"

Jackie scuffed his toe and grinned at the floor. He had never seen Mr. Hubman laugh or smile before.

Ernest turned to Dad. "There's a boy you can really be proud of, Yak. I wouldn't be surprised to see him grow up to be a minister or a yudge someday."

Otto stood forlornly by the door as everyone gathered around, getting ready to leave. Ann told again about how Jackie did all of the work himself and gave him a little hug with one arm.

Mother was right, though, the essay didn't win any *other* prizes.

DAKOTA
REINCARNATION

I was sixty-nine when I met my grandfather. It was at the Washington National Airport on November 7, 1993—the one hundredth anniversary of his death.

I'll explain as best I can.

November 7 came on a Sunday that year. During the previous week, a meeting on Dakota history was held at the Library of Congress, and I attended. Saturday evening I had dinner with Antoinette Harrington, a long-lost second cousin, at her apartment. She's a delight. Her husband died two years ago, and she has developed an interest in tracing her roots—looking at family history. I met Toni in connection with research for my recently published book, *The Nunda Irish*. The book includes a lot of family history, along with stuff about Ireland, Dakota, homesteading on the prairie, and so forth. Her grandfather and mine were brothers. They came to Dakota Territory together in a wagon train in 1876 and helped to found the Irish community of Nunda.

"Well, hi there, you black mick," she said, kissing me on the cheek. "How was your week?"

"Interesting but dull. I did get to sit by Daniel Boorstin at one of the lunches, though."

"I know you hardly ever touch a drop," she said, "but I did a favor for a couple of bigfatrepublicans a while back, and they sent me this fancy-looking bottle. I was going to throw it out, but then I thought—

Mike is coming over, maybe I can get him to share a bit of it with me?"

She was fun. *Bigfatrepublican* was all one word in our families when we were kids—I had almost forgotten. "Well, you're already holding my arm," I said. "Maybe if you'd twist it a little."

We had grilled pike, and the wine matched it perfectly. "I can't tell you how much I enjoyed your book," she said over dinner. I congratulated her on her taste and lamented the fact that the literary critics didn't share her enthusiasm to any extent whatsoever.

"Oh, literary—schmiterary," she said. "I don't care about that. It's the people. I knew that my grandfather had a brother, Jer, and that Jer had gone to the 1893 World's Fair in Chicago and died, but I knew nothing about his family."

Jer Lyons, my grandfather, was only thirty-seven when he died. Together with several of his brothers and sisters, he had taken the train to Chicago to attend the World's Fair. On the way home he stopped to visit relatives in Burr Oak, Iowa, and came down with pneumonia. It became virulent almost at once, and he died after only a few days. A telegram came to my grandmother on the farm in Dakota saying she should come because he was very ill. A second telegram, telling of his death, was delivered to her the next day while she and her children were waiting for the train to take them to Iowa.

My mother was ten months old at the time and the youngest of five children—the oldest was nine. Grandma continued to live on the farm and operate it with hired men. She died in 1943, after ten years as a wife and fifty years as a widow in that farmhouse. I knew her well because I grew up on an adjacent farm. As a single parent at the turn of the century, a time when few farm kids went beyond the eighth grade, Grandma sent all five of her children to college. She also managed her farm well enough to add eighty acres to it in 1900.

Now it was Sunday and I was at the airport, with two hours to wait for my flight back to Minnesota. As I sat in the main terminal an attractive young woman, wearing a suit that looked a little like a uniform, stepped brusquely up to me.

"Are you Mr. Mike Fleming?" she asked.

My presence was being requested in one of those rental office suites that airports now feature. She pointed out its location and left.

I was not particularly surprised. Many employees of the company I had worked for travel on business and use those airport offices. It was likely that some of my friends from the company happened to be in the airport, noticed me, and invited me to join them. I gathered up my coat and bag and went there. The door was unlocked, so I walked in.

A young man with fair hair and blue eyes sat in an armchair against the wall. He looked at me in a puzzled way. Instinctively, I was pleased to see him—I didn't know why. He looked familiar, but I couldn't place him. I pay little attention to clothes anymore, but his suit coat, shirt, and tie looked unusual to me—old fashioned, maybe. It occurred to me that he might be a visitor from one of the company's foreign subsidiaries.

"Excuse me," I said. "I'm Mike Fleming. I was given a message asking me to come to this office."

He stood and came toward me to shake hands. "I can't explain that," he said, "and I don't recognize your name, but I'm pleased to meet you because I'm altogether confused about where I am.

"I'm Jeremiah Lyons," he added, as we shook hands. Then a startled look crossed his face as he saw the effect that his words had on me.

Actually, realization had dawned on me before he even spoke his name, but it was too much to absorb immediately. My Lyons uncles had a distinctive way of speaking. They all spoke in a slow, bemused drawl. Not a Texas drawl—the Lyons drawl employed an analytical precision that dwelt on each word as though it had been carefully chosen from a thousand others to convey its message exactly. Their voices always seemed to express a friendly wonder at the vagaries of the world around them, vagaries so complex that each word and inflection had to be precisely right.

My uncles had all been dead for forty years or more, so the voice had become a distant, fond memory. Now suddenly, unmistakably, I was in the presence of that voice again.

Astonishing as it was, the voice led me to a stronger shock. I was very familiar with my grandfather's face from the picture of him I had included in my book. It was no wonder I had started back in consternation. This young man standing before me was my grandfather.

Then it hit me. Cousin Antoinette was having a little joke at my expense. I looked around the room for her in vain. How on earth had she pulled this off? This guy must be a professional actor, and the makeup must have cost a fortune. Most of all, how did they get the voice so perfectly?

It was great! I laughed and stepped forward again. "I'm quite confused too," I said, "but *very* pleased to meet you. I'm Mike Fleming, and I'm your grandson."

His eyes took in my gray hair with a quizzical look. If this was an act, it was a good one. "Where are you from?" he finally asked.

"Why," I answered, "I come from Nunda."

"Do you mean Nunda Township?" he asked, in a puzzled tone.

My idea that this was a joke suddenly looked shaky. There had been no village of Nunda during my grandfather's lifetime. It was established, and named after the township, when the railroad came through in 1910. I doubted very much that Toni even knew this; she was a second cousin and had never lived anywhere near Nunda. To her, my grandfather was a distant great-uncle who had died long before she was born, and Nunda was a name she had probably never heard until she read my book.

To all appearances, my grandfather and I were involved in some sort of a supernatural event. I hemmed and hawed and cleaned my glasses, while he scanned my face and my clothing and waited for an answer to his question. "Let's sit down here and talk about this," I finally suggested. "How did you come to be here in this room?"

That was exactly what he wanted to talk about, because he was mystified by what had happened to him. He told me about the Chicago trip, and the visit to Iowa, and his fever and illness. He had become delusional, yet he had moments when his mind cleared and he could look back on his delusions as one would upon a bad dream. Then, suddenly, he had come to, sitting in the chair where I found him. It seemed as if someone had told him to wait there, and he was doing just that when I found him. It had only been a few minutes, he thought.

"I did look through my pockets," he said. "These are my clothes, but the pockets are empty except for some cash and these strange-looking papers in my inside coat pocket." He took them out and showed them to me.

The "papers" turned out to be an airplane ticket to Minnesota on my flight. It included a boarding pass; he was assigned seat 21E. I quickly checked my own ticket and found that my seat was 21D. We were to sit together—he had the window, I had the aisle. We still had an hour and a half—and a hell of a lot to talk about. "Those are some damn funny-looking papers," he said when he saw that mine were the same as his. "What do they mean?"

"Well," I said, taking a deep breath, "I can explain what the papers are, but that seems to me to be the least of it. I think we'd better talk about some other things first. It looks to me as if you and I are involved in something very strange here. What do you think the date is today?"

"I've been wondering about that," he said. "I remember that it was Sunday, and that Dennis came in and talked to me when they came home from church, so that would have been November fifth. I remember brief episodes after that, but I think I was unconscious most of the time."

"November fifth of what year?" I asked, hoping to break the news gradually.

"Why, November fifth, eighteen-ninety-three," he answered.

I could see that my question had broadened his perspective, so I decided to plunge ahead. "This will be a shock for you," I said, "and I can't explain it because I don't understand it any better than you do. Today is November the seventh, *nineteen*-ninety-three, and I've always been told that you died on November the seventh, *eighteen*-ninety-three—one hundred years ago today."

We sat in silence and stared at each other across the table for a full minute or more. "You are right," he finally said. "That is a shock for me."

We talked for an hour or more then. I told him about the telegram that came to Grandma and the funeral and about Grandma's life afterward and about my mother and her brothers and sisters. I also told him about my book and about his brothers and sisters and other neighbors.

We had to stop talking about the past then so that I could explain about airplanes and try to prepare him for the trip back to Minnesota. He wanted to see his farm in South Dakota, of course, so we decided we would stay at my place in Minnesota overnight when we got back and then drive my car to Nunda. "What is a car?" he wanted to know.

"Let's talk about airplanes first," I suggested. "We're going to get on one soon and it would be a lot better if you had some concept of that first."

"All right. What was that word again?"

"*Airplanes*," I repeated.

It was a good thing we had been afforded the privacy of that airport rental office for the past hour. It had given him a chance to get his feet on the ground. Now I could see that he was making a transition. The family relationship helped him put trust in me, even though it involved a thirty-seven-year-old grandfather and his sixty-nine-year-old grandson. He had no idea of how he had come into this situation, but his demeanor told me that he was ready to play it out in the very best way he could.

He eyed me quizzically—almost impertinently, half-smiled like a poker player, and hitched his chair closer. "Well, let's get into it then," he said. A man who will go off to Dakota Territory in a covered wagon is not a stranger to adventure, nor is he timid in the face of it.

The explanation about airplanes went easier than I had expected. He had heard of gliders towed by locomotives, and the Chicago Fair featured exhibits by people trying to develop propeller-driven planes. I compared modern planes to ships and railroad cars in terms of size and speed. He was more than impressed, but he got the idea. I only had time to explain about the gates, and the covered ramps that connect them to the plane; then we had to get out of that office and into 1993.

"There'll be a lot of people milling around," I warned him.

He laughed. "I just came from the Chicago World's Fair."

It went well. I could see that he was astonished by the crowd, but he was more interested than abashed. He carried himself with a dignified reserve, but his face had such a good-humored, friendly look that it offset his formal bearing. It was November, but Jer still had traces of a farmer's brown neck and arms. He was about my height, just over six feet, but not as heavy. His light-brown hair was curly and combed back in a style that didn't look particularly out of place. Under it, his fair skin set off a pair of eyes that were startlingly blue.

I saw him look away and blush a little at the public displays of affection of a few couples we passed. Otherwise, he seemed to enjoy the sights of the crowd as though he had been expecting something very different, and here it was.

We held our boarding passes in our hands and moved along with the crowd into the plane and found our seats. The airport service vehicles buzzing around outside his window attracted his attention immediately, and we talked about cars and highways until the plane pulled away and began to taxi out to the runway. "It's like a real flat and wide paved road, a couple of miles long," I told him. "They have to pick up a lot of speed before the plane can leave the ground and start to fly." He looked dubious and then awestruck as we gathered speed going down the runway.

I think I saw fear in his face as we started to lift off, but that was the only time. The pilot went into his steep climb, causing the wide Potomac River and the city of Washington to appear and spread out below us. "Holy H. Smoke," said Jer as the plane banked and turned, exposing a new view. "Would you look at that! It's the Washington Monument and the Capitol. Just like in pictures."

We flew into the overcast, and then through the clouds and into bright sunlight above them. It's a strange world up there—no earth in sight, only billowy clouds far below that look as if you could walk on them. I thought he might be wondering if this had something to do with heaven, so I hastened to explain that it was only clouds and that they would probably thin out later so we could see the ground again.

I wanted to get back to 1893 and to some speculation about what was going on. He did too, but he was distracted by his surroundings. After the clouds cleared and we could see the ground, he was utterly absorbed in looking at cities, farms, roads, lakes, and traffic. The landing at the Minneapolis-St. Paul airport captured his entire attention, and the ride on the shuttle bus to the off-site parking lot was tense, but at least it gave Jer a little preview of highway traffic.

Finally, we were in my car and alone again. "This is quite a machine," he said.

"Yeah."

I've got a little Geo Metro with a straight stick, and I stopped in the open area outside the lot after I paid the attendant. I showed him the gear positions and the clutch and the accelerator.

"It looks like the same idea as the clutch on a pump jack or a horse-power," he said.

"You've got me there," I answered. "I've seen horsepowers in muse-ums, but the only one I ever saw in operation was a one-horse job that John Flynn used to run his grain elevator during threshing. I was only a little kid and didn't understand the details of it."

"Are you talking about Tom and Ellen Flynn's boy, John?" he asked.

"Well, yes, I am," I said, "but I don't think of him so much that way. He was close to sixty when I knew him."

We both mulled that over, and then we looked under the hood of the Metro. Jer was astonished at how small the engine was. He reached in and moved his hands over the parts of it. I had him stand back for a moment while I started it up so that he could watch it run and listen to it. The only basis for comparison he had was the steam engine; he knew quite a bit about the steam engines on railroad locomotives. The rubber tires on the car were an additional source of amazement for him.

It was a good thing we had the experience of the ride from the airport to the parking lot, because the ride home in heavy traffic was a white-knuckle experience for Jer. I was busy driving and he was busy hanging on and trying to look calm. It is amazing that we have as much confidence in other drivers as we do. Tons of steel routinely hurtle by us, inches away. Finally, we got off the main highway and on the rural road that leads to the farm near Stillwater where I live.

We were both glad to get there. It's a big, old, remodeled farmhouse set among several barns and outbuildings, some of which are from his time. I live here alone now. My wife died five years ago, and the kids all have homes and families of their own. For some, my place has come to seem like a tomb most of the time, but I like it. It has been home for nearly forty years.

I do a little tree farming, so I have two tractors and other equipment. Within an hour, Jer was comfortable around the place. It was warm for November, and I showed him how the tractor worked, especially the three-point hitch and the plow. I even took it out and plowed a short furrow for him, while he walked alongside and watched the sod slide up over the moldboards. We talked about some of the other equipment; he was impressed by the tree spade and the brush hog.

I felt as if we had a lot in common. He had plowed with oxen and, later, with horses. I had plowed with horses as a boy, and now I was demonstrating, for him, a diesel tractor that used hydraulic draft control to maintain the plow at the right depth. It was fun, although it seemed a little frivolous—as if we were playing hooky from some important mission we had been assigned.

It was getting toward evening, so I heated up some pizza in the microwave, and we had a couple of beers together. "Not bad," he said of the pizza, but we both felt that we didn't want to waste much valuable time on mundane subjects. I was periodically seized by a feeling that we should hurry lest this opportunity be snatched away, but I also had the feeling that I might destroy everything if I pressed too hard.

Jer didn't see it that way so much. We should just go ahead, play out our parts on this stage, and see what happened, he thought. It might take a while.

Finally, as it grew dark outside, we were able to settle down and talk. The house was warm, so he had taken off his coat and tie, and I had a better chance to look at his clothes.

I asked to look at his suit coat. It was single breasted; the cut was not really a lot different from a single-breasted sports jacket, but the material was a good deal heavier and more substantial—it was a garment made for warmth, and for wear and tear. What really made his clothes look different, I realized, was his shirt collar and tie. The tie was wide—and unknotted—like an ascot, and the shirt collar was abbreviated and stood up. Stretched back in the easy chair, with his coat and tie off and his shirt open at the collar, he looked like anybody else.

"Tell me something more about this book you wrote," he suggested after we had talked for a while. I went to my unused living room, where many excess boxes of *The Nunda Irish* were stacked, got a copy, and put it into his hands.

"Here," I said. "Keep this. You'll find a lot about yourself in there. I hope I got things right. I did the best I could with what information I had, but sometimes I had to make things up to give the story continuity. It starts in Ireland with your parents before they were married. I had to make a lot of that up. It should be more accurate as it goes along."

He paged through it and paused at the picture section. "Hey!" he said. "There's Etta Kane, my oldest sister's daughter. They live in Chicago, I just saw her there."

I was relieved. The picture had come to me without any positive identification. Until that moment, I wasn't sure I had put the right name on it.

He turned another page and smiled. "Well, it's Mary Ann and I. These were taken the year we lived in Madison while the new farm buildings were being built. That was 1887."

"Yes," I said. "It was from that picture that I knew you in Washington."

Those pictures were copies of larger, framed prints that had hung in Grandma's bedroom. The picture of her shows the tall, straight girl with large dark eyes and pretty brown hair that her oldest niece had described. She is wearing a high-necked dark dress with a white lace ruff. A substantial cross on a gold chain (it almost looks like a photographer's prop) hangs at her throat over the dress.

Grandma's eyes were keen and piercing when I knew her, the eyes of a woman who had succeeded against all odds in managing her own farm. She was the bravest of women, but she was also one of the kindest and most considerate persons who had ever lived. No one left her house without some small gift—a loaf of bread, a bouquet of flowers, something from her garden—always something. Grandma's trademarks were her sunbonnet and her apron. The apron was an ever-present shield between this tidy lady and the world of barnyard, garden, and kitchen. In it she carried eggs and radishes, baby chicks, peas, toys, potatoes, oats, cobs for the fire, or an occasional baby pig.

The eyes of the young Mary Ann that gaze out of the photo Jer was studying engage the viewer directly, with a disarming sense of honesty and candor. It is almost impossible to look at the picture without being captured by the eyes.

Jer looks slightly older than Mary Ann, which he was. He is also unsmiling in the photo, but his picture conveys warmth. Those who knew him had described him as a tall, square-shouldered, and straight young man with bright blue eyes, blond curly hair, and a warm smile. I was experiencing the warmth of his personality firsthand now.

"Why," said Jer as he turned another page, "there's my farm. How could they do that?"

"Airplanes," I answered, realizing that it felt good to be comfortable enough with him to try a little joke. The picture was an aerial photograph taken in the 1920s. The trees in the grove were larger, but it was essentially the farm he knew.

The building site that Jer and Mary Ann had selected was on the top of a broad hill near the intersection that marked the center of the mile of road that their farm faced on the south. It gave a view of almost the entire farm. On this high point, the square, two-story white house was, and still is, visible for miles. It was grand for its time, and a huge red barn and other outbuildings made their farm a showplace. The house stands in ruins now, and most of the other buildings are gone entirely. Jer was set on going there, but I had misgivings. It would be a shock for him to see what time had done to his beloved farm.

Jer turned the page to the next photo, one of my all-time favorites. It shows Grandma, in her work apron, seated on the back porch of her house. Her farm buildings are in the background. With her are her dog, Rusty, and her oldest grandson, my brother Dick. It was taken in 1939, the year she turned eighty.

I sat silent as Jer read the lengthy caption. He gripped both edges of the book and held it tight, muttering, "Mary Ann, Mary Ann." Tears brimmed in his eyes, and in mine, as we sat silent for a while.

"I just can't imagine her old like that," he told me thoughtfully. "I can see it's her. She looks almost imperial—I feel a sense of awe. To think I left her to do all that alone seems impossible. We did everything together. And it's hard for me to realize that you only knew her like that. She was beautiful, always, in every way. The picture of her with me doesn't begin to show that, although it is a good likeness. You should have seen how she moved. Even from the back, she was beautiful. Everybody said so. She had such brown hair, and wore it long on her shoulders, fixed with an ivory comb—it was her own style. When she walked or ran, she glided, and her hair moved along after her like a wave.

"I must go and read this at once, I can see that," he finally said. "We'll be able to talk better afterward. Do you have a room for me? I'd like to get started reading."

I put him in a guest bedroom that had a table and chair, plus a reading lamp over the bed. He showed a momentary interest in the electric lights, and in the bathroom appliances, but dismissed them quickly so that he could get to the book. I also gave him a pen and asked him to mark passages that were in error so that we could talk about them later. He was aghast at the suggestion that he write in the book. "My mother would turn over in her grave," he said. "Don't worry, I'll remember. Anyway, I don't want to be slowed down by taking notes. I'm going to read this whole thing before I sleep."

The book isn't long; I figured about five or six hours for an ordinary reader. He said that Ellen (his mother) had never tolerated ordinary readers in her family. It was only about nine, so it seemed possible he might do just as he said. I said good night and left him there.

I was up at seven, and I found him already outside, looking at my shop and farm equipment. The sun was just coming up, and a light frost had whitened the tall grass on the fence rows. The crisp air was a delight to breathe, and the rising sun glinted through the clouds we exhaled. He had slipped on an old jacket of mine that had hung in the open shed where I kept the tractors. We were like two Dakota farmers on a fall morning in the days of my youth.

He was in the best of spirits. My uncles (his sons) had been about this age when I first remember them, and it was like being with them on the farm again. "I don't know about you, but I could do with some coffee and a plate of sausage and eggs," I finally suggested.

"I was beginning to wonder if you ever ate anything around here," he joked.

"Well, actually I eat at the restaurant in town most of the time," I admitted. "People do that a lot now. Maybe we should just do that and then get on our way to Dakota. It's about a five- or six-hour drive, so we could have most of the afternoon out there. How did you get along with the book?"

"Well, I read it all, and then dreamt about some of it when I slept. You have some things a little mixed up in the parts I know about, but it is mostly pretty accurate. Bill Tobin actually came to Dakota before we did, but he only came to Nunda Township after his sister, Julia, married John Molumby. Some of the parts of the book in Ireland, and on the ship, seemed a little artificial to me because I know the stories so well from my mother. I really enjoyed your descriptions of my brother, Will. You have him pretty true."

"You can't imagine how good you're making me feel," I told him. "We'll talk more in the car. Let's go after those eggs."

He liked the breakfast and wanted to pay for it with the money he had. We had looked at it earlier; three hundred dollars in new twenties. "Where could I have come by so much money?" he wondered. I explained about inflation and told him it was probably much less than he thought. He didn't have enough to buy even one good beef cow, I told him, and that seemed to make the point quite well.

He did have enough to buy some everyday clothes, I suggested, in case he wanted to be less conspicuous. When the waitress took our order she looked at him, grinned, and asked if he was made up as Tom Edison. He grinned back, looked at her uniform, and said that she looked a little like Florence Nightingale herself.

"See ya, Tom," she quipped as we left.

"And you keep those bandages dry," he answered.

"Well, you held your own pretty well with her," I said as we got into the car.

"I enjoyed the conversation. It was surprising that she mentioned Edison. He was featured in several exhibits at the fair in Chicago."

"If you want to, we could stop and get you some different clothes,"

I said as we pulled out of the parking lot.

"Let's think about that for a while. Anyway, I'm anxious to get to Dakota as soon as we can."

He had become comfortable with the car, and we talked continuously. A "scandal" my book disclosed had never really taken place, he told me. The Maurice Murphy that Lizzie Horan had married had not been her uncle but instead was a Canadian by that same name who had farmed the Fitzgerald place for a few years before he and Lizzie moved on to California. Sorry, Liz.

I was very concerned about how disappointed he would be when he saw the ruins of their farmstead, so I talked about what the years have done to rural Dakota in general. Two developments—the automobile and large farm machinery—have transformed it. Places like Nunda Township have fewer people now than they had in 1893, by far. Most sets of farm buildings, once the proudest mark of the busy people there, are gone or sit vacant and abandoned. In many places, only groves of bedraggled trees remain to mark the farmsteads where Jer's friends and neighbors once thrived. The one-room country schools are gone too. The prairie landscape knew only coyotes and buffalo when Jer came there. Now, quiet has descended over it again.

"Most of the people live in Sioux Falls now," I told him. "It's a big and prosperous city."

"It was only a shabby bunch of shacks when we went through on our way to Lake County to stake our claims," he said. "I'd like to see it."

When we got to the Nunda area I drove directly toward his farm. He sat intently forward, gripping the underside of the dash. Tension was also gripping my gut until I wanted to scream. Finally, I stopped by a farm a mile east of his place to orient him. I wanted to give him more of a chance to face the reality that a century had passed and had wreaked havoc on the area he knew so well.

"This is the Rei place," I said. Bridget Rei was Jer's sister.

He stared out of the car window for a long time. "Are you sure?" he finally asked. "I don't see a damn thing I even recognize."

"I know," I said. "All the old buildings are gone. It's one of the few places still occupied and kept up. All of these buildings are new within my lifetime. I want you to try to realize what time has done. I'm concerned about the shock when you see your own place. As I told you, no one has lived there for forty years."

"I know," he said. "And I thought I understood. But seeing Bridget's place addles my mind. I'm almost afraid to go on."

"Let's swing north here and go past the Mullaney and Flynn places first," I suggested. "It will be a sad experience for you, it is for me even, but I think it will help."

"Good idea," he said. "It'll toughen me up. Lead on."

We drove the four miles around the section and past the Rei place again, but this time we headed on west toward Jer's farm.

"There's the house," he said, as it came into sight when we came over the top of the hill to the east. "Even from here it looks like hell." He was much better prepared than he had been, though, despite his clamped jaw and stony face.

Jer wandered around the farmstead, eyes on the ground, apparently searching for something familiar. The only buildings standing were the house and the hog house, plus the remains of a tile silo that was new to him. The familiar foundations of the big red barn and attached stock shed, and some internal rock and concrete, were still there. He walked around and around and over and through those structures.

As we stood looking at the hog house, he told me about building it. It's the familiar type with a short vertical wall below the peak, and a row of windows there to provide ventilation and let the hot air out in the summer. The design was very common when I was a kid, but he said it was new then and had originated at the Iowa State Agricultural College in Ames. He had corresponded with them about it, and they had sent him the plans.

We had gone to the house first, but it was simply too depressing to talk about. The farmer who rents the land grazes cattle, and the cattle had gotten into the house. Part of the roof had rotted away, allowing water to enter and rot the floor, so the cattle had broken through the floor and walls in places. The animals were probably injured in the process, and the farmer had torn off some boards and nailed them across the doors and windows, in a haphazard way, to keep them out.

I started to talk about the grove and about how almost all of the trees had died too, but he didn't answer. It seemed as if he had tuned me out and wanted to be alone, so I sat on the concrete back porch and let my own memories of the place engulf me. I should have rented one of those metal detectors, I thought. When I was a little boy my Uncle John would often give me pennies. Then he would encourage me to plant them in the yard south of the house. The pennies would grow up like plum trees, he explained, and when they bore fruit I would have many, many pennies. That was about 1933, and those pennies must still be there.

I didn't go back into the house either. From a distance it still looked like Grandma's house, but the inside was an alien barn now. Grandma's house was a place we all went for Christmas—a house jammed with cousins, aunts, and uncles, a house where we all gathered around in awe as Grandma took the huge turkey from the oven of her wood-fired kitchen stove. In Grandma's house was her mysterious bedroom, with the high elegant bed and the exotic smell of pine soap. Grandma's house held a thousand memories that had no connection to rotten, broken boards and cow shit.

Here on the porch it was different. I was sitting almost exactly where she had been sitting with Dick and Rusty when that picture was taken. Dick died in 1951. I felt close to them, sitting here. For Jer that picture evoked a world that had been lost to him, but for me it let another world live again.

Jer finally came back and sat beside me, and we looked at the picture in the book. "They were sitting right here, weren't they?" he said.

"Yes," I answered. "The big granary is gone but you can see the hog house, so the person with the camera must have been right there at the head of the cellar steps."

"God! That granary," he said. "How can it be gone? Four weeks ago I was shoveling shelled corn into one of the bins."

We were silent for a while, then he turned to me again. "What in the hell do you think is going on?" he asked.

"I don't know. We've been together for more than a day, and I feel a sense of urgency—so many important things to tell you about. There's been very little chance to even talk in detail about the lives of my aunts and uncles—your children."

"I know," he said. "Your book helped a great deal in that respect. I think there's a limit to how fast I can go. I don't really feel the urgency so much. I feel as if we'll be given time to do whatever it is we're supposed to do."

That was a lot to think about, and we both fell silent. Finally, Jer roused himself. "After my mother died, my father bought that next place west," he said, pointing. "Do you know anything about him?

"Yes," I said. "He died only two months after . . . uh . . . after you did. He's buried beside your mother in the cemetery in Madison. They have a common monument, a light-colored square stone pillar about four feet tall, with her name on one side and his on the other."

"Good," he said. "That was the plan. I know the monument. Maybe we should go there and look at that and come back here tomorrow? It will start to get dark soon, and we won't have time to look around the neighborhood today."

I wondered if we should also visit the cemetery at Badus, where he himself had been buried, but I decided not to ask.

On the way to Madison, I suggested it might be a good idea if we got a third person into this so that Jer would have the advantage of another perspective. He said it depended a lot on the person. "Unless people have changed a lot more than I think they have, most of them probably wouldn't handle this very well."

You've got that right, I thought. He also decided it was time to get some modern clothes.

We worked out a plan. Sioux Falls was only about an hour from Madison, and my younger brother, Jerry, lived there. After we left the cemetery, we'd drive to Sioux Falls. I could show him the town a little bit. We would stop at a shopping mall and get his clothes, and then I'd take him to visit Jerry. He seemed to me to be just the guy we needed. Jer liked the idea that the name was still in use in the family.

It was dark when we got to Sioux Falls. I decided to go to Fleet Farm for the clothes because Jer liked my old jacket and thought he'd like to have one like it.

He was enthusiastic about Fleet Farm. I think he was more impressed with the store than he had been with the 727 that brought us back from Washington. We spent most of an hour looking through the hardware and farm equipment areas before we went to get the clothes. We found a new jacket like mine, plus jeans, a sports shirt, and Reeboks—also socks, underwear, and a belt. "You'll be twentieth century from the skin out when you get into that stuff," I told him.

He enjoyed the checkout line and paying for his purchases. Then we came out into the mall. He was carrying his new clothes in the plastic shopping bag they gave him and was anxious to find a place to change into them. We were in the big mall on West Forty-first Street, and it was very busy. It's a nice mall; they have little islands of greenery with benches where you can rest.

My hip was bothering me from being on my feet on those concrete floors for so long. I saw a sign for a men's restroom farther down the main hall, so I pointed it out to Jer and suggested he go there to change while I waited on this bench.

"Sure," he said, suddenly solicitous. I could see that it had occurred to him to think the pace we were keeping might be too much for me. "Just take it easy for a little while here. You probably won't even know me when I come back." He laughed then, clapped me on the shoulder, and headed toward the rest room with the bag of new clothes swinging in his hand.

He was in the rest room for about fifteen minutes, and I was glad for the chance to sit. The room was directly ahead of me as I sat on the bench, so I had my eyes on the door the whole time.

When he came out, he was dressed in the new clothes. He apparently had put his old clothes into the shopping bag, which he was carrying in his hand. Something was wrong, though. He seemed to be dazed. His steps were robotlike and his eyes were unfocused. Before I could get on my feet, a man stepped up to him and held out his hand. Without even looking directly at the man, Jer handed him the shopping bag and walked by.

It seemed to be a reflex action, done without thought, but the effect on Jer was astonishing. Within two steps, his trancelike demeanor vanished. He moved toward me with a purposeful stride, and his face was pleasant and alert again. It was a pleasure to see him in modern clothes. He looked great—he was the jovial, self-assured man that his contemporaries of the past century had described. Strangers greeted him instinctively, and he smiled in return.

I stood up to meet him as he approached and was shocked to see no trace of recognition in his eyes. He walked past me without pausing, still moving with that same purposeful stride.

I stood gaping after him as he moved away from me, and then I saw where he was going. A woman of about his age stepped out to meet him. They briefly gave each other a little one-armed hug and moved off together. The meeting looked for all the world like one between a husband and wife who had agreed to meet at the mall to ride home together.

I didn't get a good look at her face, but she was medium tall and wore a brown business suit. She was carrying a briefcase, and a set of car keys dangled from the same hand that held the briefcase.

They made a most attractive couple as they disappeared around a corner among a group of shoppers. She had striking brown hair that she wore long on her shoulders; it was fixed in place with an ivory comb. It was a joy to watch her walk—she seemed to glide through the crowd, and her hair moved along after her like a wave.

I stood there, stupefied for a moment, before I raced after them, fighting my way through the crowd. When I rounded the corner they were nowhere in sight, but the group of shoppers were going into a big Sears store, so I followed. Seeing nothing of Jer, I ran out into the mall again and went out the street exit to the parking lot. I ran toward a far row of cars to catch a couple that looked like them, but it was some-one else, so I returned to the mall, and to Sears.

I searched everywhere in the next half hour, including the men's room where he had changed—nothing was there. Finally, I went back to the bench and waited—and waited. I was still there when the mall closed at midnight and a guard told me to leave.

I drove to my brother's house then and pounded on the door for ten minutes before Pat finally turned on the outside light, saw me, and opened the door. Jerry was behind her, and they peered at me from sleepy eyes. "Are you sober?" Jerry finally asked. He always was the humorist of the family.

An hour and several beers later, I finished the story. Their attitude was one of tolerant good nature. "I know you writers really get into these things, but it's damn near three o'clock in the morning. Why don't we talk about this tomorrow?"

I slept like a log. When I got up, they had both gone to work and had left a note suggesting that I meet them for lunch. I wrote an answering note, got in the car, and headed back to Stillwater. Except for Jerry and Pat, no one even knew I had been gone.

I drove back out there the next spring and talked to Jer's grave at Badus for a while. I don't know if he was there, or if he heard me or not. The only other idea I came up with was to arrange to have myself buried in the plot next to him when the time comes.

Bill McDonald, who was born on a farm near Nunda, South Dakota, in 1924, is a product of the culture he writes about in *Dakota Incarnate*. After a childhood on such farms and in one-room country schools, he served in the U.S. Army in Africa and Europe during World War II, and then took advantage of the GI Bill to attend college, graduating with a double major in physics and mathematics. He married a local girl; they raised four children who are now raising children of their own.

Bill has juggled careers — in industry, as an industrial physicist; in the military, as a now retired reserve colonel; in agriculture, as a lifetime part-time farmer; and in local government. In addition, he attended law school late in life and was admitted to the Minnesota Bar in 1982. More recently, he returned to school and earned a master of fine arts degree in English, with a specialty in creative writing, from Mankato State University in 1995.

His previous publications include scientific papers as well as *The Nunda Irish*, a book-length fictionalized history of a Dakota community, and a number of poems, short stories, and essays published by local literary journals.